THE LAZARUS TR

1994

THE LAZARUS TREE

Robert Richardson

LONDON
VICTOR GOLLANCZ LTD
1992

First published in Great Britain 1992
by Victor Gollancz Ltd
14 Henrietta Street, London WC2E 8QJ

A catalogue record for this book
is available from the British Library

ISBN 0 575 05344 5

Typeset by Rowland Phototypesetting Ltd
Bury St Edmunds, Suffolk
Printed and bound by
Butler and Tanner Ltd, Frome, Somerset

For Michael and Rona

Author's Note

The village of Medmelton does not exist, in Devon
or any other county, so it follows that the people
who live there cannot exist either.

Chapter One

Throughout that summer of sensational headlines, the dead man attracted countless unwelcome visitors to Medmelton. After following the black and white sign on the dual carriageway between Exeter and Plymouth, they drove nearly three miles along narrow lanes into the valley, buzzing with macabre curiosity. They tramped through the churchyard, taking photographs of themselves standing where the body had been discovered, and bought drinks in the Raven with an air of excited apprehension, as though any of the regulars in the bar might be the killer. But they left disappointed and none went more than once; the villagers resented their presence, inquiries to locate the cottage that the man had rented were met with feigned ignorance and persistent questions aroused hostility to the point of rudeness. When nobody was arrested, notoriety faded, the stream of the curious dried up and Medmelton returned to centuries-deep isolation amid farmland, sprawls of trees and low, protecting hills. Other Devon villages wanted to attract tourists to their historic churches, gift shops and tea rooms; Medmelton wanted nothing more than its anonymity back. When Augustus Maltravers turned to follow the sign on the last day of September, more than a year after the murder, he was the first stranger to drive down the lane for weeks.

Squeezed between thick hawthorn hedges twice the height of his car, the lane was only as wide as a single vehicle and at one point he had to reverse to a passing space to allow an oncoming tractor through. He waved to the driver, but received no acknowledgement except a look that could have been surprise or suspicion. The road divided, twisted and rose, passing beneath shallow hammocks of cables linking a procession of stark electricity pylons, then the land fell again and Medmelton appeared, cupped in its hollow. Maltravers stopped by a millstone cottage and got out of the car to look. The biggest building was the church, square Saxon tower half-hidden among thick yews and tall copper beeches; just beyond was the sparkle of a shallow ford where the road crossed the Ney, a minor tributary of the Teign, before climbing again between hedged ploughed fields of dark red soil and disappearing towards the sea. Around the church and immediately beyond the ford, ancient cottages fringed an open green with newer housing forming a spreading stain into the farmland. The only sign of life was a speckle of grazing cattle on the far side of the valley. Under amber autumn sunshine, it looked the sort of place that would be disturbed by nothing more dramatic than jam-making jealousy in the Women's Institute or rivalry with another village's darts team. But, putting the murder aside, Stephen Hart's letter had hinted at something sinister, and Stephen was a level-headed, worldly-wise Londoner not susceptible to excessive imagination. He had asked if Maltravers could fulfil a long-standing invitation to visit him and Veronica and see if a detached mind could make sense of something at best ridiculous, at worst threatening. Maltravers's blue eyes squinted against light the colour of syrup as he tried to work out where his destination must be.

'Good afternoon.'

A woman had unexpectedly appeared by the wall of the cottage's front garden. Dressed in denim dungarees, she was about fifty, with the slenderness of youth ripened but not become fat, and a helmet of ash blonde hair framing a long oval face.

'Hello,' he said. 'I'm sorry, I didn't see you.'

'I was behind the wall.' Her hand holding a trowel indicated downwards. 'Weeding. I heard your car stop and thought you might be coming here.'

'No, I was admiring the view. I'm visiting friends. Can you tell me how to find Dymlight Cottage? All I know is that it's near the church.'

'Stephen and Veronica's?' The woman walked to the wooden gate, opened it and came to stand next to him, pointing with

8

the trowel again. 'Cross the ford and there's a turning immediately on your right. You can't quite see it from here. Dymlight's the last cottage you reach.'

'Thank you.' Now close to her, he could see her eyes; one was brown, the other green. 'Obviously someone born in Medmelton would know.'

'And was I born in Medmelton?'

'Somebody in the family was . . . "Young men beware, if they be wise, a maiden with Medmelton eyes."'

'I see.' Intrigued and amused, the eyes sparkled. 'A visitor who does his homework . . . or did Stephen and Veronica tell you?'

'They told me,' Maltravers admitted. 'Although I don't think you're a particularly extreme example.'

'No, I'm not. The legend runs a bit thin in me. You'll see much more dramatic ones in the village. Are you staying long?'

'Only a few days.' He held out his hand. 'Gus Maltravers.'

'Sally Baker.' She pulled off a soiled canvas gardening glove and the handshake gripped like a man's. 'I ought to warn you that you'll find yourself a novelty round here. Not many Londoners visit Medmelton.'

'And am I from London?'

She nodded towards the dealer's sticker in the rear window of his car. 'Somebody bought the car there.'

Maltravers laughed and gave a slight bow of acknowledgement. 'Touché. Are all Medmelton maidens so quick?'

'You'll find out, won't you?' Sally Baker pulled her glove back on. 'Anyway, enjoy your stay. Perhaps we'll run into each other again.' She smiled and returned to the garden.

Maltravers said goodbye and climbed back into his car. As he dropped down the hill, his mind idly ran over what they had been talking about. Medmelton eyes – the brown one usually on the right – could be traced back to 1608 when one Joan Garret had been charged at Exeter Assizes with bewitching the husband of another woman. She was sentenced to a painful flogging at a cart's end drawn through the village and nothing more was heard of her, but the eyes, turning up at random in several unrelated families, had been associated ever since with

9

the sort of girl who made parents of young men nervous. The fact that the overwhelming majority had led blameless lives and in the nineteenth century one of them had been a courageous and saintly African missionary had done nothing to ameliorate their reputation. Science had long explained the phenomenon as a genetic hangover of close relation breeding in past generations, but it was still remarked on when it occurred. Veronica Hart had them, as did her daughter Michelle, an odd but attractive feature.

Maltravers reached St Leonard's and stopped again. His journey had been quicker than he had anticipated and he was not expected for nearly another hour. As the church was apparently a central point of Stephen's concerns, it seemed worth exploring. He unlatched one half of the double lychgate and passed beneath its weather-blackened shingle roof; a red shale path ran straight ahead between the tombstones to the porch of the west door, outside which stood a sweet chestnut, helter-skelter bark twisted round its broad trunk. In the grass beneath was a small, rusty iron plaque with 'The Lazarus Tree' cast into it. It was the focal point of a highly dubious legend involving a young man who had promised to marry a girl when it bloomed on the feast day of St Leonard; as that was November 6, he didn't start planning his bachelor night. But, as he should have known is inevitable in such stories, on the appropriate morning the tree had duly been in full flower with the girl standing beneath it, ready and probably smug in her wedding dress. The original tree was long dead, but a replacement had been grown from it, and others in turn had been produced to preserve the story.

But such pretty nonsense was not the reason for Maltravers's interest; more than a year earlier, Patrick Gabriel had been found under the Lazarus Tree, not, as those who knew him might have expected, drunk, but dead from a savage knife slash which had severed his throat. Maltravers had known Gabriel slightly – they had shared the same publisher – but had not liked him. Arrogant, conceited and provocatively rude, the only thing that had made him tolerable had been his unquestioned talent; he was one of a minute number of poets successful enough to make a living from his craft. He had gone to Medmelton to complete what was to be a book-length poem which had caused excited anticipation in lit-crit circles as soon as it was known to be planned. Nobody knew why he had chosen the village, except that it was quiet and far removed from the interruptions his reputation caused in London; until his death, virtually no one knew he had gone there. Then someone had killed him, with no sign of a comprehensible motive. It had been mystery, sensation and literary tragedy, the latter compounded by the fact that his rented cottage had contained not a single line of his writing for posthumous publication. Somewhere on a police file it remained an unsolved murder, the subject of wildly speculative newspaper articles and endless gossip, frequently libellous, until it had become passé and half-forgotten.

Maltravers moved on to the church. The porch had stone seats running down each side of a wide chequered tile step with a wooden board fixed to one wall carrying notices announcing times of services, the name and address of the verger, village events and a parish council meeting and advertising the work of the Church of England Children's Society. He could explore no further as the door was locked. He walked back to his car, reflecting that television aerials and a satellite dish did nothing for the appearance of a terrace of cottages on the far side of the green. Tyres throwing up low waves as he bumped across the ford, he immediately saw his turning and followed the church-yard wall until he reached Dymlight Cottage, hidden behind a ten-foot privet hedge. Taking his suitcase from the boot, he opened the gate and walked through the garden; outside the open front door a teenage girl lay on a faded sun lounger, transistor radio playing pop music turned low next to her. It was still warm enough for her to be wearing shorts, slender legs crossed at the ankles, and a sleeveless scarlet T-shirt under which disturbingly mature curves rose and fell with drowsy breathing. Spiky black hair was cut short and the youth-hollow face was disguised by sunglasses, worn more for effect than necessity.

'Hello, Michelle,' Maltravers said.

'Mmm?' The girl sounded irritated. 'What is it?'

'It's not a what, it's a who. Follow the sound of my voice.'

She turned her head without raising it, one hand pushing the glasses on to her forehead. 'Oh, hi. They're inside somewhere.' The glasses covered the eyes again and she abandoned what temporary attention she had paid him. He went in search of a more enthusiastic welcome.

Dymlight Cottage had been built solid and functional in the 1870s for a farmworker and his family; one large, all-purpose downstairs room with a scullery at the back, two bedrooms and a midden in the garden. More than a century and a great deal of money later, all that the Victorian tenants would have recognised were the outer stone walls and preserved, if now purely decorative, chimney stack. Bits had been ripped out, added on, adapted, converted, enhanced and occasionally ruined. The scullery had been in turn woodstore and utility room, its primitive facilities long overtaken by the gadgetry of a picture window kitchen extension at the back. The cottage had grown sideways and upwards to provide a second down-stairs room, third and fourth bedrooms and upstairs bathroom (the malodorous midden was now a toolshed). Changing tastes had produced successors to the original blackleaded fireplace including a mercifully long gone tiled version in the style of a 1930s semi-detached, a pretentious imitation stone monstrosity circa 1955 and now a brick-lined inglenook in which stood a hammered copper cauldron filled with an eruption of dried flowers; heating came from radiators, architecturally idiosyn-cratic but thin enough to be unobtrusive. The front door still opened into what had been the single downstairs room, stone walls painted soft green above the mahogany brown parquet floor. Among the furnishings, only the television and CD player were modern; the dining suite, sofa, occasional chairs, display cabinet and bookcases had been garnered from antique shops and house auctions, with nothing later than the turn of the century.

Opposite him was the door into the kitchen and Maltravers could see Veronica at the sink under the window overlooking the back garden. Black as her daughter's, her hair hung loose almost to her waist, vivid bougainvillaea flowers printed on her Indian cotton dress half-hidden by its coal-dark, gleaming waterfall. He had made barely any sound, but she seemed instantly to sense someone was there and even who it was.

'Hello, Gus.' She did not move for a moment. 'Good journey?'

'Fine. Even had time to stop and look at Stonehenge.'

He put down his case and she finally turned as he crossed the living room. With its high forehead and long nose, her face at first appeared plain until its individual, slightly stern beauty struck you, enhanced by the striking eyes. As they kissed – she had to raise herself only fractionally to his six-foot height – he felt again the quality which had struck him the first time they had met. Veronica had an uncanny self-control. Her emotions never showed and he had found it almost impossible to reach her as a person. She was not unfriendly, but always gave the impression in any conversation of doing no more than politely stepping out of a private shell. There was a sense that if Stephen and Michelle were suddenly to die, she would not feel the anguish of being alone because she always was alone, protected by barriers that could not be breached. They probably went back to her childhood, but it seemed that she had gone into total hiding behind them when her daughter was born. Even now, nobody knew who Michelle's father was.

'Where's Stephen?' Maltravers asked.

'In the loft. Why don't you go up? You can put your things in your room. It's the last door along the landing. I'll make some tea.'

The greeting was typical. Apart from the briefest inquiry about his journey, no questions, no idle chat to make contact. Veronica did not start conversations, she only responded to them; her talk, like her actions, was basic and practical.

His room was in the rear of the extension, with a view across the interlocking hills rising towards the main road. He left his case to unpack later and went back to the landing from which an aluminium folding ladder led up through the loft entrance in the ceiling.

'Permission to come aboard,' he called as he started to climb the steps and his head appeared through the hole. The loft had been completely floored and was illuminated by neon strip lights fixed to the roof beams. Stephen Hart was sitting at a desk, working through a pile of exercise books. It was difficult to analyse how he simply looked like a schoolteacher, but he did. Tall and gangly in stone-washed jeans and corduroy shirt, he retained the air of a radical student, an impression enhanced by the close-cropped beard, darker than his now unfashionably long reddish hair. He turned to Maltravers, brown eyes alert behind gold-rimmed glasses.

'Hello, Gus. Welcome to the back of beyond.'

'And a very pretty back of beyond,' Maltravers commented as he stepped off the ladder. 'People take photographs of places like this and wish they lived here.'

'Mind the beams,' Stephen warned as he straightened up. 'Stay in the middle and you'll be all right.'

They had first met at a weekend literary workshop when Maltravers had been called in at the last minute to replace a rather more successful television writer who had been taken ill. In the bar one evening, they had started discussing the Brontës – Maltravers had suggested they were an example of bad parenting rather than genius – and had gone on to Hardy, Dickens and Somerset Maugham, concluding that weird childhoods created the best writers. Several beers later, Maltravers had claimed Hampshire as England's greatest county because it had produced both Jane Austen and cricket; thereafter the talk had been of Sobers, Cowdrey and Botham, classic batting rather than classic literature, and a friendship had begun. At the time, Stephen had been an English teacher in Hornsey, near enough to Maltravers's Highbury flat for them to meet regularly and spend afternoons at Lord's and the Oval. One evening, Maltravers and his partner Tess Davy had invited him to join them at a Sondheim charity concert at the Theatre Royal, Drury Lane and he had asked if he could bring a girl he had met on holiday. She was Veronica Dean and Tess had told Maltravers that evening she was convinced they would marry; less than six months later they did, Stephen finding a job at a comprehensive in Exeter and moving to Veronica's cottage in Medmelton. Apart from a couple of visits to London by Stephen, Maltravers had not seen them since the wedding.

'Veronica's making tea, so we ought to go down,' Maltravers

said as they shook hands. 'I met Michelle on the way in. How old is she now?'

'Fifteen going on twenty-five,' Stephen replied caustically. 'When she goes off to the disco in Exeter, she's jail bait.'

'I can imagine it. A friend of mine once said you're getting old when you realise you're old enough to be the father of something you fancy. Crude, but accurate. What does Veronica think about it?'

'That's still the forbidden country,' Stephen said. 'I soon learnt not to try and invade. There's a private line between those two and nobody else gets on the wavelength.'

'Perhaps women with Medmelton eyes are like Midwich Cuckoos. They know each other's minds.' Maltravers was only half joking; secret and incomprehensible, the relationship between his wife and his stepdaughter had troubled Stephen for a long time.

'I sometimes think that. Did you notice Michelle's eyes? They're not the usual way round. She has the green one on the right.'

'Is that meant to be significant?'

'It's the mirror image and is very rare. The old wives' tale is that everything is reversed in women who have it. Good is bad, Hell is Heaven, the Devil is God. They're all meant to be left-handed as well.'

'Is Michelle?'

'She's ambidextrous.' Stephen grimaced. 'Close enough.'

'Whoever teaches biology at your school should be able to explain it without any difficulty. All I can remember about Mendel's Law is that it started with him playing around with peas, but it means that I've got blue eyes and am right-handed. There's no great mystery about it.'

'I know all that, but you've got to take Medmelton super-stitions on board as well. There are legends – and a lot of people believe them.'

Maltravers shrugged dismissively. 'I don't know how many traditional old wives you have around here still turning out instant eye of newt and wing of bat soup, but I've seen a satellite

dish, so the late twentieth century appears to have reached Medmelton.'

'Believe me, Gus, I sometimes wonder about that.'

Against all reason, it would not be long before Maltravers
would also be having doubts.

Chapter Two

'Have you ever heard of Ralph the Talespinner when you've been in Devon before?' Stephen asked as they drank their tea at the kitchen's pine refectory table. Veronica was preparing a casserole cooked in beer – she had taken little part in the conversation since they had come down – and Michelle was still outside trying to preserve the suntan from their Greek summer holiday into an English autumn.

'Never heard of him,' Maltravers replied. 'Who is he?'

'Was,' Stephen corrected. 'Village idiot or rustic genius, depending on your point of view. Born in Medmelton about 1720 and never left the place all his life. You name it, Ralph had a story about it. Did you see the grooves in the north wall of the church when you drove up?'

'Didn't notice them.'

'About twenty feet off the ground, now known to be caused by some geological fault in the stone. According to Ralph, it was all the work of the Medmelton Cat.'

'The Medmelton Cat,' Maltravers repeated.

'That's it. Look out of your bedroom window and a mile or so down the valley there's a small hill. Put your imagination into overdrive and you can convince yourself it looks like a cat curled up asleep. Ralph's tale was that at midnight on New Year's Eve it woke up, came into the village and sharpened its claws on the church wall.'

'Did they leave a saucer of milk out for it?'

'No, but any virgin – you know the sort of Freudian hang-ups all these stories have – who was not indoors would be eaten by it.'

'Dragons had similar tastes,' Maltravers commented. 'I'd have thought any intelligent girl would have done something about her condition as soon as possible to have herself taken off the menu. The word must have got around that it was a fate considerably better than death. What else did Ralph come up with?'

'You name it. Misty castles that appeared once a year, endless ghosts, some Arthurian knight who wandered in from Cornwall, flying giants, two-headed unicorns, assorted witches – and that a group of Bronze Age standing stones were seven maidens who had been instantly ossified for dancing on a Sunday. The stories were all collected and published. We've got a copy somewhere. I'll try and find it for you.'

'I'll make it my bedtime reading,' Maltravers said. 'I might find some ideas I can steal.'

Veronica put the casserole in the oven. She had given the task all her attention, but was now ready to talk.

'When's Tess arriving?' she asked.

'Two or three days,' Maltravers said. 'Depends how long she's tied up in Bristol doing these voiceovers for the BBC Natural History Unit. Doesn't pay much, but it's better than resting. Good acting parts haven't been thick on the ground lately.'

'We saw her in the television adaptation of *The Country Wife*,' Veronica added. 'She was marvellous.'

'So when's the big break coming?' Stephen asked.

'You can't make that happen,' Maltravers replied. 'It either does or it doesn't. Tess isn't bothered. She's offered enough work to be able to choose the parts she likes, which makes her a damn sight luckier than most. She nearly landed . . .'

He was interrupted by a woman erupting through the kitchen door from the back garden. Small and slender with what would be a pretty face when not flushed frantic pink, her chestnut hair appeared not to have been in the neighbourhood of a comb since she woke up that morning.

'Veronica! Panic!' She was as agitated as a startled bird. The crisis sounded at least of local earthquake proportions. 'Have you got any red wine?'

'Yes, Ursula. Calm down.' Veronica's assurance carried

echoes of similar dramas in the past as she opened the pantry door. 'How much do you need?'

'Only enough for coq au vin. I could have sworn I had some, but when I looked . . .'

'Here you are.' Veronica handed her a half-full bottle. 'Got everything else?'

'I think so. I was halfway through preparing it when I realised. Thanks. You've saved my life again . . .' She suddenly stopped and looked embarrassed as she saw Maltravers. 'Oh, sorry, I didn't realise I was interrupting.'

'I told you we were having visitors,' Veronica said. 'This is Gus, a friend of Stephen's from London. Gus, Ursula, my sister-in-law.'

'Hello.' Maltravers stood up and held out his hand. She held out the hand still holding the bottle, then agitatedly corrected herself.

'Hello. Nice to meet you. How long are you . . .' She let go of his hand as though it was red hot. 'Oh, God! I left everything on the kitchen table! The cat'll be eating it! I must get back. Thanks, Veronica.'

She fled in the same whirlwind state as she had arrived, clutching the wine as though terrified of dropping it. Totally unaffected by the visit, Veronica began to fold a tea towel as though the incident had not occurred.

'I hope the cat leaves something,' Maltravers remarked.

'She's only next door,' Stephen told him. 'It's probably not even in the house, anyway. Ursula lives in perpetual crisis. She constantly expects the worst to happen, so it usually does. We're used to it. There's an obvious explanation as to why she had no wine as well. Anything alcoholic lying around in that house tends to disappear.'

'Gus isn't interested in family gossip,' Veronica said quietly.

Maltravers saw the warning glance she gave her husband; she was clamping a tight lid on his conversation. Ursula drank, which Veronica would see as weakness. People with such inner strength, their emotions straitjacketed, often found it impossible to comprehend – or forgive – any inability to handle life. It was a stupidity, dismissed as not worth thinking about. Diplomatically, he changed the subject.

'I could do with stretching my legs,' he said to Stephen. 'How about the fifty-pence village tour?'

'Sure.' Stephen finished his tea. 'Dinner about seven is it?'

'Yes,' Veronica replied. 'See you later.'

Finished in the kitchen, she left the room and went upstairs to tackle whatever was next in her organised life. Maltravers and Stephen went out by the front door; Michelle did not acknowledge them or even move as they passed.

'I don't think I said thanks for coming,' Stephen said as they walked alongside the church wall. 'It's getting heavy round here and I felt I needed some help.'

Raised so immediately, Maltravers reflected that whatever had caused Stephen to invite him was obviously as serious as he had concluded from the letter. Sometime student union president at a redbrick university, assistant to a left-wing Labour MP and energetic fundraiser for War on Want, Stephen Hart had been the classic radical whose firebrand youth had burnt out. To the faithful, he had sold out, but others would say he had done no more than grow up. He had ceased to be hot-headed and become level-headed – and should not be alarmed by things that on the face of it struck Maltravers as little more than mischief.

'How long has whatever it is been going on?' he asked.

'It began in May, although at first I didn't take any notice.' Stephen smiled sourly. 'It seemed harmless then. I couldn't put all the details in my letter, so I'll fill you in from the start.'

They had reached the road through Medmelton and Stephen led the way across the narrow pedestrian path over the ford to St Leonard's lychgate.

'You know about the Lazarus Tree where Patrick Gabriel's body was found, don't you?' he asked as they entered the churchyard.

'Yes. In fact I stopped to look at it when I arrived.'

'Well, that's where it's been happening.' They reached the sweet chestnut and Stephen crouched down, indicating a crevice where the trunk sprang from the ground. 'Bernard Quex, our rector, found a cheap plastic doll here. Sort of thing you can buy in any shop. What made it odd was that a moustache had been painted on it.'

'Some toy that a child had lost?' Maltravers suggested. 'Most kids have paintboxes and decorate things.'

'Possibly,' Stephen agreed as he straightened up. 'But it appeared to be brand new. Its price label was still on it.'

'What did your rector do?'

'Mentioned it casually to a few people then forgot about it.'

'Did he keep the doll?'

'Yes, and it's now part of quite a collection. A lock of hair, an old scent bottle with what looks like dried blood in it and a bunch of wild flowers all turned up in the same place.'

'Are you sure it was blood?' Maltravers asked.

'Not positive, although I could take it to school and have one of the science staff test it.'

'Well, it's certainly worth confirming. It could be anything ... but even if it is blood, it could still be nothing more than children's games, couldn't it? Local kids dabbling in what they think is witchcraft. Comes of reading too much Stephen King at a susceptible age. They grow out of it.'

'I know they do,' Stephen agreed. 'But this has been going on for four months. Kids aren't usually that consistent. They mess about with these things for a while, then lose interest.'

'Any pattern to it? Always on the same date of the month for instance?'

Stephen shook his head. 'No. It seems to be done during the night because the last time it happened, Bernard had been out late and walked past the tree around midnight. He's certain there was nothing there then, but the flowers were there in the morning.'

'It might not be in the night,' Maltravers pointed out. 'If it's some kid who lives nearby, they could slip out and do it first thing in the morning.' He looked at Stephen closely. 'I need some more input from you here. You've not asked me to Medmelton just to talk about silly games in the churchyard. What's really worrying you about this?'

Stephen stared at the hiding place at the foot of the tree for a

few moments. 'I'm worried that Michelle could be mixed up in it.'

'And what makes you think that?'

'I saw her here in the churchyard a couple of evenings in the summer. She wasn't doing anything, but this isn't the sort of place she comes to. She hangs around with other kids or goes to their homes to play records. She stopped having anything to do with the church long ago.'

'Did you talk to her about it?'

'Yes, but it was a waste of breath. She just clammed up.'

'What about Veronica?' Maltravers asked. 'Is she worried?'

'No. I asked her to talk to Michelle, but she said it wasn't anything important.'

'Perhaps she's right.'

'And perhaps she's not. I know you're thinking I'm being irrational, Gus, and I wish I could convince myself I am. But it's . . . I don't know. Medmelton's schizophrenic. Picture postcard village, but full of things you can't put your finger on.' Stephen waved his arm at the gravestones surrounding them. 'There are people buried here who go back to Tudor times and you can find the same names in today's telephone directory. There was no running water here until the 1930s and it's only since the Second World War that outsiders from Exeter have started moving in. This place was isolated in a time warp for centuries.'

'Oh, come on,' Maltravers protested. 'There are hundreds of villages just the same. I know places in Norfolk that have hardly changed since the Domesday Book. But they haven't opted out of the twentieth century. Don't try to tell me Medmelton doesn't watch *Neighbours* or hasn't heard of Madonna or Gazza. Has moving to the country addled your brain?'

'No, it hasn't,' Stephen replied firmly. 'But superstitions ruled here for a very long time and there are people alive who can remember Medmelton when it was still like that. You and I have had discussions about old magic and you didn't dismiss it out of hand.'

'No, I didn't,' Maltravers agreed. 'But this looks no more than kids messing around. Kids who buy pop records and trendy clothes. Living in Medmelton probably bores them stiff, so they make a bit of excitement for themselves. I'm sorry, Stephen, but you're not being logical.'

'But you still came after I wrote to you.'

'Your letter didn't spell out the details and I thought there was something serious.'

'But now you don't think it's serious.' He sounded disappointed.

'Frankly, no.' Maltravers held his hand up to stop Stephen speaking again. 'But hold on a minute. I'm talking the way that you would have done before you left London. So either you've started to go mad or . . .'

'Or something else is mad?' Stephen said quietly.

'Something else is certainly odd. But explainable without things that go bump in the night – and in any case what do you expect me to do about it? If you can't get to the bottom of whatever it is, why should I be able to?'

Stephen shook himself as though frustrated. 'I'm not sure. Perhaps because you're not as close to Medmelton. This isn't going to make much sense, but after we moved here I started to become . . . involved. It's a lovely village and it was marvellous living in the country. And I was crazy about Veronica. There's an almost mystical side to her, incredibly still and secret. I wanted to try and reach that, so I began to let myself be absorbed in this place to understand her better. I became . . .' He stopped. 'Christ, I can see it in your face. You're trapped in a country churchyard with the village idiot.'

'I'm in a country churchyard with someone who is highly intelligent and not frothing at the mouth,' Maltravers corrected. 'You're right, it doesn't make much sense, but when I last saw you around the beginning of this year, you were still rational and perfectly normal. Now you know you're not being rational and are worried enough about it to ask me if I can help. I don't know if I can, but I think I should try.'

'Thanks, Gus.' Stephen looked relieved. 'Ever since you agreed to come, I've been trying to work out how to explain it without you calling for men in white coats. I feel like that woman in *The Cocktail Party* who asks the doctor to tell her she's mad because if she isn't it means that the world is mad and she couldn't stand that.'

'I don't think you're mad,' Maltravers assured him. 'But the world can be – anyone who reads political history knows that – and Medmelton might have its share of insanity.' He looked down at the grass beneath the Lazarus Tree. 'And what about the fact that Patrick Gabriel had a moustache and his body was found here?'

'That's what makes it worrying.'

Maltravers took out his cigarettes and offered them to Stephen who shook his head. 'Sorry. I'd forgotten you'd given up. Spare me your lectures.' He lit one thoughtfully. 'Has anybody *any* idea who killed Gabriel? Or why?'

'No,' Stephen replied. 'Only that it was almost certainly somebody local. Medmelton doesn't attract visitors, even in the height of summer, and it's almost impossible that a stranger wouldn't have been noticed. I was one of the people questioned by the police for no more reason than that I'd chatted to him in the Raven a few times. As far as I could make out, there wasn't the smell of a motive and precious few clues.'

'But now odd things are happening where his body was found . . . so what do the police think?'

'They haven't been told. Bernard insists there's no need. I don't think he wants the church to be the centre of another scandal.'

'For God's sake!' Maltravers protested. 'You're dealing with an unsolved murder here. The police aren't going to be best pleased when they find that something's been happening that might be connected – however unlikely it may seem – and it's been deliberately kept from them. Sod all around your rector's feelings, why haven't you gone to them?'

Stephen looked defensive. 'Because I'm worried about Michelle, Gus. I have to know how far she's involved – if she is involved – before I do anything.'

'That's a luxury you can't afford and you . . .' Maltravers glanced at him with a sudden sharpness. 'Hang on. Are you thinking she was mixed up in the murder?'

'I'm trying not to,' he replied levelly. 'But I think she may have something to do with these things beneath the tree and . . . well, that's the problem, Gus. I don't know what to do.'

'Stephen, if Michelle's playing strange games and if they could be even remotely connected with Gabriel's death, then . . .' Maltravers shook his head impatiently. 'It can't be kept a village secret because you don't like it.'

'Who murdered Gabriel has been kept secret,' Stephen pointed out. 'I'm convinced some people have suspicions, but they haven't told the police about them. It's that sort of place.'

'But if somebody knows anything that might help solve a murder, they have to tell the police. You know . . .' Maltravers broke off in frustration. 'For Christ's sake, why am I having to spell this out to you?'

'You don't have to spell it out, Gus,' Stephen replied. 'I know. I just need you to help me through it.'

They stared at each other for several moments, then Maltravers broke the silence. 'I'd like you to buy me a drink. Suddenly I need one. And we seem to have a lot to talk about.'

As the two men left the churchyard, Michelle rolled out of the lounger as the last of the afternoon sun moved off her. She stretched lazily and looked across to St Leonard's through the gap where the gate broke the high garden hedge and saw them passing under the lychgate. Flinty and suspicious, Medmelton eyes glittered like a lizard's.

Chapter Three

Nature had not been kind to Mildred Thomson. In her childhood, people had remarked on her energy and constant laughter, diplomatically avoiding any comment on her looks. As she grew up in a generation which had neither invented the word nor recognised the concept of a teenager, even the most charitable had to say she was . . . different; the less charitable bluntly called her ugly. Increasingly conscious of her appearance, she became resentful of other girls, any one of whom seemed pretty in her presence. During the Second World War, she lived away from Medmelton for the only period in her life, working as a canteen assistant in Plymouth dockyard, where sexually frustrated sailors outnumbered available and co-operative females. The word rapidly spread that when all else failed there was always Mildred – and all else failed constantly. Peace ended the job and with it a time of pleasure and satisfaction. In 1946 she returned to her parents' all-purpose shop and for the rest of her life went no further from Medmelton than Exeter and occasional return visits to Plymouth. By the time her parents died, she had become as much a part of the village as the Memorial Hall, which was also unlovely, functional and taken for granted.

But Plymouth had left a sour aftertaste. Between nineteen and twenty-four, Mildred Thomson had enjoyed the attentions of men, something she would hardly ever know again. Her contemporaries flirted, dated, and were chased; Mildred sliced bacon. Then they married; Mildred threw confetti and cried herself to sleep after the one occasion when she caught the bride's bouquet. Then they produced daughters; Mildred sold them boiled sweets. Then the daughters married and Mildred was no longer invited to the weddings. Then the daughters had daughters and all of them were pretty. Memories of brief happiness turned sour and quietly rotted into bitterness and resentment. Emotional needs that could not be fed turned inward and consumed her.

Then she began to detect the dissatisfaction among the teenagers hanging around the village, bored with its monotony, convinced that if they could only escape to Bristol or London or *anywhere*, life would become exciting. There was nothing to do in Medmelton — until Mildred offered something forbidden, guarded like a thrilling secret. Because only a carefully selected few were allowed to know it. And of that few, Michelle Dean was special. Granddaughter of a woman who had hurt Mildred with unthinking adolescent cruelty years before, father unknown, Medmelton eyes reversed, daring, rebellious and with the ability to keep silent about anything.

'What an extraordinary looking woman,' Maltravers commented as he and Stephen walked away from Medmelton Stores where he had stopped to buy more cigarettes.

'You mean Mildred?'

'That woman in the shop. I hate to be unkind, but I've never seen anyone quite like that before. When she speaks, her mouth stays still and her face moves.'

Stephen laughed. 'Sorry. We're used to Mildred's looks, but they are a bit off-putting at first. She's all right.'

'Is she married?' Maltravers asked as they crossed the green towards the Raven.

'No,' Stephen replied, 'although everyone believes she's worth a packet. She inherited the shop from her parents and it's a gold mine. You'd think someone would have been prepared to put up with her looks to get their hands on the money.'

'Maybe she didn't want that,' Maltravers commented. 'But when nature's been that unfair, you have to find some compensations. What are hers?'

'Classic gossipmonger, I expect,' Stephen said. 'The shop's a focal point of the village, so everybody knows Mildred. She can be moody sometimes, but who can blame her?'

They reached the pub and Maltravers followed Stephen into

the lounge bar. Dating back into hazy time, the Raven had remained unchanged for centuries until it fell victim to a brewery combine's modernisation programme. Broad oak floorboards sprinkled with sawdust had been swept and covered with fitted carpet; the tough texture of granite walls smothered with plaster; evocative dirt-aged beams cleaned up and painted; a plain wooden counter where one could imagine characters out of Hardy drinking rough cider replaced with an anonymous polished bar, brass fittings and padded stools duplicated in thousands of other pubs. It had been sacrilege in the shape of the corporate plan, spawned of a mentality that would put plastic thatch on Anne Hathaway's cottage. Maltravers looked at the labels clipped to a row of imitation pump handles, all offering beers he would refuse in London, and settled for a glass of wine. Bland melodies recorded by bored session musicians seeped through the sterile room.

'O brave new world,' he groaned as they sat down. 'Where's the Space Invader machine?'

'There isn't one,' Stephen told him. 'They tried it, but most people still played dominoes and cribbage.'

'There's hope yet . . . anyway, let's get back to Patrick Gabriel. Do you *seriously* think Michelle was mixed up with his death?'

'I think she could be mixed up with this nonsense under the Lazarus Tree – and that obviously could be linked to Gabriel,' Stephen replied. 'I know it's bizarre, but I don't think I'm being irrational.'

'All right.' Maltravers discovered that his wine was better than he had expected. 'Let's start with Gabriel. Did Michelle have anything to do with him while he was here? Where did he stay, incidentally?'

'He rented a cottage next to the rectory behind the church. It belongs to some friends of his in London,' Stephen told him. 'I don't *know* if Michelle had anything to do with him, but it's possible. He often wandered about the village and was prepared to talk to anyone.'

An ugly possibility crossed Maltravers's mind; Michelle would have been only about fourteen at the time Patrick Gabriel was staying in Medmelton . . . he kept the thought to himself.

'Is she interested in poetry?' he asked.

'In certain poets – and she likes Gabriel's work.'

'They'd have got on like a house on fire, then. Gabriel thought that everyone should fall down and worship his genius.' Maltravers did not like the way in which the unpleasant thought returned. 'But, even so, it's a hell of a jump from them talking to each other to her knowing something about his death.'

'Of course it is,' Stephen acknowledged. 'But nobody knows anything about Gabriel's death, so everything becomes possible. Most of us were as mystified as the police. There was no apparent reason why anyone should kill him and rumour took over. It became a sort of challenge to come up with any theory more excessive than the last one. If you believed them all, just about anyone in Medmelton could have done it. The weirdest one I heard was that the rector was mixed up in it.'

Maltravers looked amused. 'And what was the basis for that?'

'I can't remember now.' Stephen leant forward on the table. 'It was crap anyway – and most of the other theories weren't any better – but everything suggests that Patrick Gabriel was murdered by someone from this village. And until I know who it was and why they did it, I don't know who else could have been involved. And that now includes Michelle. I don't like that, Gus, but I can't ignore it.'

Maltravers remained silent for a few moments, absently splitting open the edge of a beer mat with his thumbnail. Stephen needed reassurance, but without more information it was impossible to give it to him.

'Fill me in on the details of the murder,' he said finally. 'I've forgotten most of them.'

'Details are scarce anyway,' Stephen replied. 'Gabriel was apparently killed at the Lazarus Tree – there was no sign that his body had been taken there from somewhere else. The police combed the churchyard, but didn't come up with anything. It was in the middle of a dry spell and the ground was bone hard. They never found the weapon, although . . .'

'Just a minute,' Maltravers interrupted. 'I remember reading that the body was found in the morning, but when was he actually killed?'

'According to the police, between midnight and one o'clock.'

'So what was he doing in the churchyard at that time . . . and who knew he'd be there?'

Stephen shrugged. 'Join the guessing game. He was drinking in here until just after eleven, then he certainly went back to the cottage because he telephoned somebody in London about eleven thirty. This all came out in the press reports.'

'Anything significant about the phone call?'

'Not as far as I know. I think it was to his agent. Funny time to call.'

'Typical of him,' Maltravers said. 'He kept to his own clock and expected everyone else to adjust to it. Did the police turn up anything in the cottage?'

'The only significant thing was that the poetry wasn't there. There were several sets of fingerprints and they wanted to know who they belonged to. They finally set out to fingerprint everyone in Medmelton – it wouldn't have been difficult, it's a small enough place – but there was too much resistance.'

'You mean people refused?'

'The police can't force you to let them take your fingerprints,' Stephen pointed out. 'There were endless arguments about it in here and a lot of people wouldn't have anything to do with it. They got uptight about being suspected.'

'But they weren't suspected,' Maltravers argued. 'It was just elimination.'

'I know that, you know that. They weren't having it.'

'So how many wouldn't co-operate?'

Stephen shrugged. 'I don't know exactly, but a lot. Telling the police to get lost became something to boast about.'

'I assume that you co-operated.'

'Yes – but Veronica didn't. She just said it was nothing to do with her. She wouldn't give permission for Michelle either. It was as though . . .' Stephen hesitated, '. . . either as though finding who killed Gabriel wasn't important or that outsiders shouldn't interfere.'

'A murder inquiry is hardly interference,' Maltravers commented.

'Not everybody thinks like that in Medmelton.' Stephen finished his beer. 'I'm going to have another half. Same again? We've got time.'

'Thanks.'

More customers had arrived and Maltravers watched Stephen greeting them at the bar. There was the instant camaraderie of people who inhabited a small, insular world, elliptical remarks incomprehensible to an outsider. It was unremarkable enough; pubs in even the most densely populated areas of London had coteries of regulars sharing a localised identity. But in Medmelton it ran deep, jealously guarded to the extent of defying outside authority. Had any of those who refused to co-operate with the police done so because they knew something which they had decided should go no further? A resentment of outsiders taken to extremes? Fulfilling Stephen's request that he should try and find something out could run into very solid walls. Absorbed with his thoughts, he did not register as someone else came into the pub and paused by his table.

'Hello again.'

For a moment, the name would not come back, then he remembered. 'Hello. Sally Baker. The directions were perfect. Thank you.'

'It's not hard to find ... Can I buy you a welcome-to-Medmelton drink?'

'Thanks, but Stephen's getting them. Would you like to join us?'

'I'm meeting someone. Another time though.'

She crossed to the bar where she also was welcomed by several other customers, including Stephen who had just been served. Maltravers mentally noted that Sally Baker had again shown that she at least was not hostile towards strangers.

'That's the woman who gave me directions when I arrived,' he said as Stephen rejoined him. 'We met outside her cottage. She seems friendlier than what appears to be the norm around here.'

'Sally's been tainted by the outside world,' Stephen told him.

31

'She was born here, but her husband was some big wheel at the Foreign Office and was posted all over the place. She came back about five years ago after he died. She's settled in again – on the parish council and very active in the church – but she actually knows that if you drive beyond Exeter, you don't fall off the edge.'

Maltravers grinned. 'A definite sophisticate. Anyway, back to Gabriel. He'd been here about a month when he was killed, hadn't he? He must have made some sort of contact with people during that time. Did anything particular happen that was . . . I don't know . . . suspicious?'

'Not that I know of. He bought basic necessities at the stores and came in here most evenings. People were a bit distant at first, but thawed out when they found he was always good for a drink.'

'But he wasn't the easiest person to get on with,' Maltravers commented. 'I'll rephrase that. He was an obnoxious sod on his good days. I can't imagine him sinking a few in here and not picking a row with someone.'

'If he did, I never heard about it. I chatted to him myself a couple of times and he was all right. I knew his poems and was interested in what he was working on.'

'Well, as long as you were suitably adulatory, you'd have been all right. He was convinced he was a genius – and in fairness, he could be that good – and was always ready to talk about himself. Did he tell you anything about the poem he was writing?'

'Not in detail, but he said it was about love. Profane, romantic, forbidden, divine, you name it. It was going to develop the *Rage in Passion* collection. Have you read that?'

'Of course I have. Some of his best work is in it.' Maltravers frowned. 'I wonder where he was taking it?'

'More to the point, why did someone steal it? He said he used a series of notebooks. One for ideas, one for first drafts, one for second, then another for the final version. There wasn't a single one in his cottage. It doesn't make sense.'

'Unless someone intended to try and pass it off as their own later.' Maltravers dismissed the suggestion as quickly as he

32

raised it. 'But that would never work. Gabriel's style was as distinctive as Hopkins's sprung rhythms. Anyone would recognise it.'

'So why were the notebooks stolen? The obvious assumption must be that the theft was connected with his death. And where are they now?'

An interpretation of 'Just the way you look tonight' played with all the lyricism of a Gregorian chant floated out of a loudspeaker above Maltravers's head. Stephen was not thinking certain things through because he didn't like where such thoughts might lead. He was obliquely asking to be made to face them.

'Have you searched Michelle's room?' he asked quietly.

'No.' Stephen looked away. 'But I ought to do that, oughtn't I?'

'Yes, and you know it. But I can understand why you don't want to. How frightened are you about what you might find?'

'Try terrified.' Stephen sighed. 'Veronica's turned off, everybody else wants to forget it and I can't hack it on my own. Look, Gus, just tell me I have to do it and perhaps I'll be . . .'

'No,' Maltravers interrupted. 'If you haven't been able to convince yourself of that, there's no reason why I should be able to. My best offer is to ask questions as a vaguely inquisitive tourist and see if I unearth anything. I'm not promising results – talking to strangers isn't the done thing round here – but people can do nothing worse than tell me to get lost. Unless it's always open season on writers in Medmelton.'

Maltravers suddenly became aware of Sally Baker again. Sitting on a bar stool at the far side of the room and paying no attention to the man talking to her, she was looking straight at him; she held his eyes for a moment, then turned away.

As she finished setting the table for dinner, adjusting a place mat, fractionally moving the Georgian silver cruet, Veronica's uncertainties reawakened. Stephen had never really explained why he had suddenly been so keen for Maltravers to visit them. Of all his friends, she had liked Gus and Tess the most for their acceptance of her, their instant respect for the limits of how close they could approach. But she recognised that Gus had been intrigued, the writer in him watching for signs that would explain her personality. And when he had telephoned after receiving the letter, Stephen had almost insisted that he must come. Afterwards he had been evasive; a visit was overdue, it fitted in with Tess's coincidental work in Bristol, it was just time they came. But this was not the moment to invite outsiders to Medmelton, not when so much was creeping back to the surface, so much that had been kept quiet for so long.

Upstairs in her room, Michelle held the key tight in her fist as she thought; finding different places to hide it had become part of the secrecy. First she had cut a hole in the pages of an old book, then it had been taped underneath the frame of her bed, then tucked into the toe of a shoe. There was no need for such precautions; even if her mother or Stephen realised that the cupboard in her white bedside unit was always locked, they would assume it contained something personal and both of them had always respected her privacy. But she still had to be careful. This time the key could go in the pocket of her sundress, washed and hung away for next summer. As she dropped it in, she remembered letting Nicky's skilful olive fingers slip the straps off her shoulders in her hotel room that afternoon in Naxos. Nothing had happened, because they had been interrupted; Steve had wanted to complain to the hotel manager, but her mother told him to forget it. And afterwards Nicky had moved on with the indifference of a languid Greek satyr, amused and satiated by an endless supply of eager girls. For the rest of the holiday Michelle had watched them – Claire from Lyons, Carol from somewhere in the Midlands, Lise from Copenhagen – faces flushed with excited guilt betraying them whenever he appeared. Nicky used them like he had nearly used her and she hated that; it made her as stupid as the rest of them. Back home in Medmelton, she had poured out that hatred to Mildred, the only person who really understood that Michelle Dean was different.

Chapter Four

Ursula Dean twitched as she heard Ewan arrive home; it was twenty to seven so he must have been held up by traffic out of Exeter. As the car door slammed, she stood up, eyes anxious about the living room. Neatly folded, the *Daily Express* lay on the table next to his chair ready for him to read; dulled silverware which he had commented on that morning now gleamed; fresh chrysanthemums filled the china vase on the window ledge. Nervously convinced something had been forgotten, she went into the kitchen and took a can of beer from the fridge and began to pour it. Her hand shook and she guiltily rubbed away a few drops that splashed on to the quarry-tiled floor with a soft-soled slipper. As she finished, she had another panic attack. Throw away the can immediately or leave it until she had put his glass by the newspaper? Every day brought a series of moments of similar uncertainty, commonplace domestic actions exaggerated into crises. Something inside her knew it was ridiculous, but she stood in the middle of the room, staring at each hand helplessly, unable to decide. As Ewan walked through the kitchen door, the glass shook as she twitched again. He glanced disapprovingly at a fresh scatter of drops on the tiles, then strode past her without a word and she heard him go upstairs. Ursula went back into the living room and put the glass on the table, ready for him when he had changed.

In its newly polished frame, a wedding photograph on the pine shelves he had built into the wall mocked her with its lost, now almost impossible to believe, image of happiness. Ewan had been the handsomest boy in Medmelton, sleek black hair, features clean cut as a Galahad; slim and vivacious, Ursula had been pursued by him and all his friends. When they became engaged, her mother had said there would be a lot of broken hearts in the village. But fifteen years had tarnished the gloss; passion had lost its fire and become ashes instead of warm embers, the shared anguish of not being able to have children had changed to a sense of inadequacy and incompleteness on her part and resentment on his. He had turned away from her; at first she had been sure he had sublimated it all into running the model shop, now she was convinced there was another woman in Exeter. Lonely and unhappy – Ewan's mother had never worked and he would not allow his wife to do so – Ursula drank. She was thirty-seven and felt on bad days like the grand-mother she would never be; he was forty, body still hard and lean, and could beat men half his age on the squash court. On the now rare occasions they went out together, other women's faces flashed interest as they nudged their friends, slyly nodding towards him. Not that he ever showed any response. Like Veronica, he had inner control, brother and sister sharing impen-etrable, unnerving self-possession.

'It's coq au vin for supper.' The sentence spilled out the moment he came back into the living room, not casual infor-mation but an offering seeking longed-for approval. See, I am a good wife; I mind my house and care for my husband. An indifferent nod was her token reward as he sat down and opened the newspaper.

'Busy at the shop?' Now see, I am interested. You won't let me work there, but I want to be involved.

'Fairly.'

'You're later than normal. Was the traffic bad?' Now I am concerned about your welfare. Please recognise that.

'Heavier than usual.' He folded the paper at an article that had caught his attention and picked up the beer. He did not look at her.

'I . . . I did the silver.' Don't ignore me. I'm your wife.

'Good.' The absent response sounded as though he was approving of something he was reading rather than what she had done.

Depressed by his rejection, Ursula went back into the kitchen and began to lay the table. I do my best. I don't want to be despised. I try not to drink. I want to be valued. I do not want to hate my husband. I want him to talk to me and to listen. I want to be loved by him because I think that I still love him.

And I don't know how long I can live with the guilt of what my desperation has driven me to doing.

'I must ring Tess to let her know I arrived in one piece,' Maltravers said.

'Phone's in the front room,' Stephen told him.

'No need. I'll get my portable from the car.'

'Portable?' Stephen mocked. 'Keep it with the Filofax, do you? Never thought you'd become a yuppie.'

'The yuppie is extinct, although there are reports of fossils being dug up in Sloane Square,' Maltravers replied. 'And there is no Filofax. I have no wish to live my life in fifteen-minute segments hoping I'll be famous in one of them. I only have the phone because I won it in a raffle. Took me three weeks to discover how the damn thing works. Back in a minute.'

He remained outside to make the call, leaning against his car and looking across at St Leonard's.

'Having fun?' he asked.

'Fun?' Tess repeated cautiously. 'Not quite the right word. I am incredibly well informed on the life cycle of *Pediculus humanus* – the human louse to you – and have become neurotic about keeping clean. Tomorrow it's sex among the tortoises.'

'Does the earth move for them?'

'Yes, but *very* slowly. How are Stephen and Veronica?'

'Fine, apart from Stephen worrying about his stepdaughter. Some odd things have been happening.'

'Serious odd?'

'They could be.' Maltravers noticed the grooves he had been told about in the church wall. 'The trouble with Medmelton is that it's got more superstitions than can be consumed locally. Even the woman who owns the village shop looks like a witch.'

'She can't help her looks.'

'True. Anyway, the point is that whatever's going on is getting to Stephen.'

'Think you can help?'

'I'd like to, but I'm not sure how.'

'Well, I'll be there soon and you can tell me how you're getting on. Don't get turned into a frog in the meantime. Look, I must dash, I'm going out to dinner with some of the production team. Miss you.'

'Miss you too, lady. Take care.'

They rang off and Maltravers slowly pushed the telephone's aerial back into place. Tess had been a contrasting voice of normality after an unexpectedly disturbing couple of hours in Medmelton. There could be explanations for what had happened which might be unexpected, even outrageous, but were nothing to do with either the supernatural or an unsolved murder. The fact was that Stephen was simply not thinking straight. *If* Michelle was responsible for putting a weird collection of things under the Lazarus Tree – and there was no proof of that – it did not automatically follow that it was anything to do with Patrick Gabriel's death. So she could have done it because . . . well, in Medmelton anything appeared possible. According to Stephen, the place was so thick with malevolent enchantment that . . . Maltravers slammed home the last inch of the aerial in annoyance. He was holding modern technology in his hand and beginning to think like a medieval peasant. Medmelton could be pinned down on a map, it was part of a local government authority, some MP sought its votes, its church roof probably needed repairing and it was full of people who had overdrafts, collected soap coupons and took holidays on the Costa del Sol. Now somebody was playing games and . . . his eyes sharpened as he caught a movement in the churchyard. Michelle was standing with her back to him by the Lazarus Tree. He dropped the telephone on to the passenger seat through the car window, then stepped across the narrow lane and vaulted over the low wall. The girl made no movement as he silently approached on the grass between the tombs.

'Hello.'

She whirled round and her look shook him. She was not just startled at being disturbed, her face held the fury of a suddenly trapped animal. The expression instantly vanished as she ran her fingers through cropped hair as if needing to make some sort of movement.

'Oh, it's you. I didn't know anyone was here.'

'What are you doing here?'

'Minding my own business.' She stepped away from the tree and kicked a pebble which pinged against a weather-worn gravestone. 'Nothing wrong with that is there?'

'Of course there isn't,' Maltravers replied. 'Are you interested in the churchyard?'

'No.' The denial was very sharp, and before he could speak again she glanced at him inquiringly. 'You live in London, don't you? Whereabouts?'

'Highbury. Have you heard of it?'

'Don't Arsenal play football there or something?'

'Not far away. Do you support them?'

The girl shrugged. 'A boy I know at school does. I'm not interested . . . is it anywhere near Blackheath?'

'No. That's the other side of the river. Why do you ask?'

'No reason. What's it like, living in London?'

'Fine if you like big cities. What's it like living in Medmelton?'

'Like being dead.' She kicked another stone, this time to emphasise the statement. 'I just want to get out. I want to go to London.'

'Perhaps you will one day. When you're older and . . .'

'Don't you start,' she interrupted. 'That's what everybody says. I'm old enough now.'

Maltravers surprised her by agreeing. 'Yes, I rather think you are. But there are boring laws about being under age. You run off, and they'll drag you back. Pisser, isn't it?'

'Worse than that.' Her voice held an echo of the anger he had seen moments earlier. 'Is dinner ready?'

'I imagine so.'

'I'd better get back then.'

She turned and ran towards Dymlight Cottage, not waiting for him to accompany her. Maltravers watched her leap over the wall with teenage ungainliness and disappear through the garden hedge. Frustration over living in Medmelton was irrelevant; most of her contemporaries in the village would share it.

So her interest in London was natural enough – but she had mentioned Blackheath, which was where Patrick Gabriel's house had been. Stephen said he had seen them talking together, so Gabriel could have mentioned it and it didn't necessarily mean anything. Except that more than a year after his death, it remained in her mind. And that brought back the disagreeable thought that had come to him in the Raven.

'Thanks.' Maltravers accepted a pewter tankard of beer that Stephen had filled for him. 'Tell me more about Sally Baker. Has she remarried?'

'No.'

'Why not? She's an attractive woman.'

'And comfortably off,' Stephen added. 'Foreign Office widow's pension on top of everything her husband left her. But she's happy enough on her own. Works part-time in Exeter Library and still travels a bit. There's a married daughter in Scotland she's always visiting. We'll invite her for a drink while you're here.'

'Look forward to meeting her again.' Maltravers indicated his plate as he looked across at Veronica. 'This is very good. Traditional Devon recipe?'

'No. Out of a cookery book.'

'Another disappointment,' he joked gloomily. 'Friends of mine in the Lake District once served up Lancashire hotpot from a book with all the instructions in French. At this rate, all the English will have left will be fish and chips. And you can't get them wrapped in newspaper any more. Although I remember seeing someone eating chips from a story I'd sweated blood on when I was working in Worcester. I felt quite depressed about it.'

He steered the conversation away from Sally Baker, but had decided that he wanted to talk to her again. Her connection with St Leonard's meant she must be aware of what had been happening and her knowledge of the village might shed some light on what were becoming increasingly dark corners.

Michelle went out again as soon as the meal was over, and chat, half-watched television and a few drinks filled the remainder of the evening for the rest of them. She returned about ten o'clock, vague about where she had been and what she had been doing; Veronica appeared indifferent and cautious inquiries from Stephen were dismissed or ignored before she went to bed. They stayed downstairs talking, and it was nearly midnight before Maltravers turned off his bedside light. Contrasting with the familiar traffic noises subconsciously heard and ignored through the night in London, Medmelton was filled with hollow country quietness. The bed was a maddening two inches shorter than his six-foot frame, and he lay awake in discomfort, during which time he discovered that the silence outside was constantly punctuated by tiny high-pitched squeaks, translated by imagination into a terrified slaughter of small creatures. And the house creaked . . . and the beer had reached his bladder.

His bare feet made no sound on the landing carpet as he went to the bathroom; a strip of light gleamed at the bottom of Michelle's closed bedroom door and as he passed he could hear her speaking. Did she have a phone in her room and was she having a late-night chat? No, there was something about her voice, not conversation with natural pauses, but controlled and deliberate as if reciting a mantra. He held his ear close to the door, straining to hear. The voice rose and fell, only fragments of what she was saying audible.

'. . . us suffer eternal judge . . . ears merciful . . . justly art sins . . . for seek we may . . .' Maltravers leant closer as her voice dropped again, then, '. . . born is that man.'

There was no more, and moments later the light went out. Maltravers quietly returned to his room. Using the lavatory would have to wait until he could be sure she was asleep and unaware that someone might have heard. Switching his own light on, he found his diary and wrote down what he had caught, then underlined 'eternal', 'merciful' and 'justly art'. Too antique for Michelle's everyday vocabulary, so she had been quoting something. The rhythm had been wrong for poetry circa the sixteenth century being committed to memory for homework, but that had been its flavour. Maltravers was hazy on prose from that period except for the King James Bible or Cranmer's Book of Common Prayer, which he read for glowing language rather than theology. If it was from either of those, he did not recognise it – and they were not what he would have expected Michelle to read aloud in bed. Stephen would know what she was studying in English which might provide a clue, but Maltravers remembered the tone of her voice. Deliberate, demanding . . . and sinister? Or was that just the after-effect of mysterious little noises in the night?

Michelle was also still awake, uncurtained windows admitting the light of September's last moon. She felt as she always did after doing something childish, annoyed that her knowingness could still fall victim to games in which excitement temporarily masked their stupidity. So why did she play them? Not because she shouldn't. There had been endless things she had done which were like that. She could even remember the occasion when she had first lied as a little girl. It hadn't been an important lie, but after she had told it she had been aware of the realisation that the instinct always to tell Granny the truth could be ignored. Other children could no more recall that moment in their lives than they could remember taking their first steps, but Michelle did and it had been an important moment in discovering the secretive and special side of herself. She had Medmelton eyes reversed, there were things about her that nobody in the whole world knew; she was different. So perhaps they weren't childish games after all, perhaps she was the only one with the ability to play them. And that *was* exciting.

Chapter Five

Monday morning school regulation grey pleated skirt covering her knees, plain blue blouse, white ankle socks and flat black shoes gave Michelle the air of a sullen captive in prison uniform. Her conversation was reduced to monosyllables, her resentment tangible; she followed Stephen out to the car like an animal temporarily tamed to obedience but liable to turn wild again without warning. Her mother and stepfather treated her behaviour as normal, overriding sulky protests, going through a regular litany over the contents of her schoolbag, dinner money and PE kit. Maltravers's goodbye was not even acknowledged with a grunt.

'How's she doing at school?' he asked when he and Veronica were alone.

'Well enough when she tries. It's just a matter of keeping on at her. I was the same at her age.'

Maltravers reflected how little he knew about Veronica's past. She had taken a polytechnic catch-all sociology course before briefly working in a local authority social services department. She had been twenty-two when Michelle was born and after that had lived with, and presumably been supported by, her parents; if there had been any financial help from Michelle's father, it had never been admitted. When Stephen had met her, she had just begun her part-time job with a community youth project in Exeter. She revealed nothing about her experiences, people she had known, things she had done, presenting an image as basic as the bare essentials on a business card. Maltravers knew other people like that and they were as humdrum as they appeared. But with Veronica there was the sense of a real face behind the mask, scarred by experiences, passions and hurts. Her self-containment could be uncomfortable and was always uncompromising. Gentle probing brought deflection, anything stronger and the barriers came down. It was a quality she had passed on intact to her daughter.

'When do you have to leave for work?' he asked.

'I catch the bus outside the Raven at nine o'clock. What are you going to do for the day?'

He glanced out of the kitchen window. October had begun mild and sun-filled. 'Wander round Medmelton. Play at tourists. I might drive over to Buckfast Abbey later.'

'Try the George for lunch,' Veronica suggested. 'I must get ready.'

Maltravers finished reading the paper after she left, then sat in the front room, thinking over what had happened. The objects left in the churchyard were open to all manner of interpretation and imagination could run riot. Sally Baker's knowledge of Medmelton still made her the best – in fact, the only – person he could think of to discuss that with. He took out his diary and re-read what he had heard Michelle saying during the night. '. . . born is that man.' A real man? Some traditional catechism to charm out the identity of a lover? Romantic country lore advised girls to peel an apple carefully then throw the whole skin over their shoulder when it would land in the shape of their true love's initial; there were countless similar superstitions. But a phrase like 'eternal judge' sounded a gloomy way of summoning up Mr Right, and anyway such an attempt was totally out of character with Michelle. He recalled a phrase from Saki: 'Children with Hyacinth's temperament don't know better as they grow older; they merely know more.' He suspected that Michelle already knew more than she should, but with the conceit of adolescence had convinced herself that she could handle it.

He was interrupted by the front doorbell and went to discover a tall, rather crumpled clergyman. The navy blue suit needed pressing and was worn over a chocolate brown pullover and grubby dog collar. The tidiest thing about him was his Brylcreemed black hair, cut severely short with no pretension to style, smears of grey just above the ears like patches of ash on partly burnt coal; his face was of a young man prematurely aged, combining innocence and benevolence with world-weariness. His regular features would have been handsome if they had not all been slightly too large. Heavy closed lips widened into what should have been a smile, but only managed to look like a patronising smirk.

'Ah, you must be . . .' he paused momentarily. 'Gus . . . Maltravers, is it? Stephen mentioned your name to me.'

'Yes. And you must be Bernard Quex, rector of this parish. Stephen mentioned your name to me. Good morning.'

'Good morning . . . have I missed Veronica?'

'I'm afraid so. She left for work about a quarter of an hour ago.'

'Oh, I forgot that she goes in on Mondays. Could you ask her to ring me when she gets back?'

'Of course. I'll leave a note in case I'm out.'

'That's very kind.' Quex clearly felt that he could not just end the conversation there. 'You're staying for a few days, I believe.'

'Yes. I finally found time to accept the invitation. I'm looking forward to discovering Medmelton.'

'I hope you won't be disappointed.' Quex smiled disparagingly. 'It's very attractive, but not remarkable. The church is the only interesting building, but there are dozens exactly like it all over Devon.'

'But they haven't all had murder victims found in the churchyard.'

The remark was made casually, but had an instant effect on Quex, as if Maltravers had uttered an obscenity during a Mother's Union meeting.

'That was a long time ago and it's over now.' He sounded both wary and offended. 'It was very . . . embarrassing and we don't talk about it.'

Maltravers noted the preferred adjective. Not tragic, not wicked, not mysterious, but embarrassing, as though Patrick Gabriel had committed a *faux pas* by inconsiderately being murdered in the village and giving Medmelton a bad name.

45

'Hardly over,' he commented blandly. 'There's still the question of finding the person who did it.'

The ripple of offence at being contradicted that crossed Quex's face was instantly replaced by a condescending and pious smile.

'God knows, Mr Maltravers. There are no secrets from Him.'

The capital letter was as audible as the tone of conviction and Maltravers instantly recognised there would be no point in arguing.

'Interesting though,' he added. 'However, nice to meet you and I'll make sure Veronica gets the message.'

'That's very kind.' Quex's amiability resurfaced, but Maltravers felt that he was now suspicious of another stranger from London. 'Enjoy your stay. Good morning.'

As the rector turned and walked away fractionally too quickly, Maltravers remembered what Stephen had said about his attitude towards the things he had discovered beneath the Lazarus Tree. That the police should not be involved because Medmelton had been disturbed enough without a murder inquiry being resurrected. Somewhere in the village – possibly somewhere among Quex's congregation – there was a killer, but he was deliberately holding back evidence that might identify them. For the greater good of the parish or because he knew something? Perhaps because he was turning to the touchstone of unquestioning faith in God. Maltravers made a mental note to ask Stephen if Quex had been among those who had refused to co-operate with the police's fingerprinting operation. If he had . . . no conclusions yet, just bear it in mind.

He scribbled a note for Veronica, then left the cottage and strolled past the church and across the green. The walk to Sally Baker's would be good exercise, but he did not have to take it; she stepped out of the door as he was passing Medmelton Stores.

'Hello,' he said. 'This is almost serendipity.'

'What is?' she asked.

'Meeting you. I was on my way to your place to see if you were in.'

'What for?'

'Because apart from Stephen and Veronica, you're the only person I know here and I need some help.'

She regarded him quizzically as she shifted a wicker shopping basket from left hand to right. 'You only arrived yesterday and already you need help about something? You struck me as being more . . . capable.'

'I am when I know what I'm dealing with.'

'I see . . . well at least I can save you a walk. My car's just across the road.'

'Here.' He held out his hand for the basket. 'Let me carry that.'

'Is it something to do with Michelle?' she asked unexpectedly as they started to walk towards the car.

Maltravers glanced at her in surprise; Sally Baker was both astute and direct. 'And how would you know that?'

'Educated guess,' she replied. 'I was watching you and Stephen in the Raven last night. Instead of him introducing you to everyone at the bar, you were sitting on your own and obviously discussing something serious. Not the sort of behaviour I'd have expected when you'd only been here a couple of hours.'

Maltravers nodded approvingly. 'You don't miss much. But why should it have anything to do with Michelle?'

'Has it?' she repeated.

'Yes.'

'Well then.' She took the car keys out of the pocket of her Barbour jacket. 'Tell me about it.'

It took only a few minutes to reach her cottage and Maltravers completed his story while she unloaded the shopping in the kitchen.

'I'm not altogether sure why I'm talking to you,' he admitted when he finished. 'If I had to rationalise it, I'd say that you know this village as well as anyone, but you're not as insular as a lot of people here. But spelling it out makes it sound a bit thin, I'm afraid. Perhaps it's because my cosmopolitan mind can't cope with country matters.'

'Maybe it can't.' The agreement sounded ambivalent. 'But I'm very grateful that you've talked to me. Let's go into the other room and I'll tell you something.'

Sally Baker's front room was unexpectedly exotic with African tribal masks, Indian bronzes, carved ivory figures and embroidered pictures of Japanese wildlife. A Chinese tapestry screen stood in one corner and the sideboard was dominated by an ebony box, its lid inlaid with gold swirls of leaves and lacquered flowers.

'Stephen mentioned that your husband was in the diplomatic service,' Maltravers remarked. 'I see you picked up souvenirs.'

'Some not by choice,' she said drily. 'It was out of the question to decline gifts from certain people, but I was awfully glad when we were able to get rid of a shrunken head from Nairobi. They said it was an immense privilege to be given one, but it always looked so incredibly reproachful. Anyway, let's talk about superstitions nearer home.'

She sat in a very English wingback chair and was silent for a moment. 'I knew about the things under the Lazarus Tree, of course, but . . . well, first of all, you need some local history. Donkey's years ago, there was a man called Ralph the Talespinner, who . . .'

'I've heard of him,' Maltravers interrupted. 'The Medmelton Cat and God knows what else. Stephen's got a copy of his stories somewhere.'

'Which edition?' The question was unexpectedly sharp.

'I don't know. Is there more than one?'

'Yes. And I'll bet his is the 1933 version. That's the most common.'

'Does it matter?'

'Very much.' She twisted round in her chair, reached towards an open bookcase built into the wall beside her and pulled out a book bound in faded purple leather. 'Ralph was a reasonably good storyteller, but he was illiterate and they could all have been lost or mangled by verbal tradition if the rector at the time hadn't written them down. In 1890 one of his successors had them published by a printer in Exeter.' She held up the book. 'This is a copy, and I know of hardly any others.'

'How does it differ from the 1933 edition?'

'This one's complete. It contains everything the first rector wrote down, including some half-finished tales and a collection of Ralph's sayings, none of them memorable. When it was republished, it was edited. The sayings went and half a dozen stories were left out, including . . .' she flicked through several pages then stood up and handed him the book, '. . . this one. It's quite short. I'll make coffee while you read it.'

She left the room and Maltravers heard her opening cupboard doors in the kitchen as he started to read.

Mary of Medmelton and Her Pact with the Lazarus Tree

There was in the reign of Queen Elizabeth a maiden of Medmelton called Mary Twelvetrees, fair and comely and beloved of all menfolk. But she was fickle and taunting with her favours, now allowing one to believe he had won her, now giving her attentions to another, now to a third and to a fourth. In this way, she found amusement and flattery, taking all manner of gifts and tokens, but never giving her heart or affections in return.

But, unlike the endless Blessings of Heaven, all earthly happiness is but vanity when best achieved and of the Devil when gained through selfishness or pride and Mary found that the young men grew weary of her and turned their attentions to others less beautiful than she but of kinder nature. In vain did she then flaunt herself and make promises in which all knew she would prove false until at last she reached the age of twenty years and was still without a husband. At about this time, there arrived in Medmelton a Cornish man seeking work and he became the servant of a farmer. He was without a wife, which was a great wonder, he being well-proportioned and of handsome countenance. On becoming acquainted with this man (who was called Arthur of Redruth, that being the place from whence he came), Mary decided upon him for herself and vowed to act with swiftness in her purpose ere others in Medmelton should advise him of her past conduct. Accordingly she attended upon him, making him gifts of needlework and victuals, affecting a becoming modesty which had been no part of her character heretofore and doing all things pleasing to a man. In this manner, she succeeded in wooing and winning him and by the festival of Easter they were betrothed.

But just as it sometimes pleases Almighty God to exact just penalty for sin within a man's mortal span rather than allowing him to attend the torments of Hell that await all sinners, so it was that Mary was to be denied love as she had cruelly withheld her own from others. For it came to pass that Arthur was stricken of a malady swift and terrible and died within three days of its commencing. Weeping greatly, Mary sat by his corse, witnessing in its lifelessness the very death of her own hopes. She remained in this lamentable state for several weeks and did then betake herself to a woman of Exmoor skilled in the black arts. The woman did advise her to make a pact with the Lazarus Tree that grows hard by St Leonard's Church, saying that the blessings that fell upon the maiden who found her husband by its miracle could also be hers. Forasmuch (said the witch) as the tree returned to life in the same manner as the dead brother of Mary and Martha in Scripture, so too could Arthur be returned to her.

The next, immensely long paragraph abandoned the story as it listed with relish the alarming and painful consequences of denying God and dabbling in witchcraft. Maltravers realised he was reading Ralph the Talespinner with added sermons from the rector and skipped over the solemnities to pick up the story again.

Satisfied by the woman's words (and not knowing their deceit), Mary returned to Medmelton to carry out the charms and practices she had advised. Secretly and at night, she knelt by the Lazarus Tree as others knelt before the Cross of Calvary, perverting worship of Our Blessed Saviour into sinful and wicked promises if the tree would return her love to her. Having thus placed her immortal soul in deadly peril, she began to carry out strange and unnatural acts, laying beneath the tree (as it were in the form of offerings) several items as she had been instructed. First she placed a figure made of clay in the form of the dead man; then a lock of his hair which she had cut from his head; then a phial of her own blood; then her betrothal ring; then a posy of white campion, mallow and speedwell; each time praying according to various devilish forms. When she had done all these things, she most wickedly cut from a book of Holy Writ those passages written by the Apostle Luke telling of the miraculous Raising of Lazarus by Our Lord Jesus Christ and left them beneath the tree also. Then she returned to her home and waited, for the witch had told her that Arthur would rise up and come to her when these things had been done. For three days and nights she took neither meat nor drink nor any sleep, until on the third night about the hour of midnight, there was a great knocking at the door of her cottage.

Full of joy (for her desires had conquered all conscience of what she was about) she leapt up and opened the door, then shrank back in fear and trembling, for before her stood Arthur of Redruth wrapped in his burial shroud and bearing still the marks of his terrible last disease.

'Mary! Mary!' he cried aloud and in great anguish. 'Why didst thou do this thing? For now I am taken from the bourne of Heaven itself and returned to Earth neither mortal man nor Angel which I was.'

Then did he turn from her and fly like a spirit into the waters of the Ney where he was turned into the great stone in the likeness of a man which stands in the river by Tom Blackwall's Meadow. And as she saw it happen, Mary threw herself after him, clinging to the rock as a bride clings to her husband, wailing greatly that the sound was heard as the howling of a wolf for twenty miles around. And the Ney being in flood, she was wrenched from the rock by the power of the water, even as she had torn Arthur from the bosom of God, and her body was washed down and down unto the sea where (it is said) her cries of misery are still heard each year when the wind blows on the night of her death.

Therefore those who hear this tale beware, that they might turn their thoughts from all things that are evil and abhorred of God . . .

Maltravers stopped reading as the rector added a final admonitory message. Sally Baker had returned with the coffee.

'Hear any echoes?' she asked.

'Obviously, but . . .' His mouth twisted dismissively. 'Come on. This is just a fable to frighten the children with a bit of free preaching thrown in. It might have had them trembling in their shoes in seventeen-whatever, but it's only got novelty value now.'

'For most people,' she agreed. 'For grown-up people. But how straight did you think when you were fifteen?'

'I was past fairy stories,' he replied firmly.

'And because you were past them, is everybody? There are adults who believe that what they see in television soap operas is real.'

'But not to the extent of living their lives accordingly,' he argued. 'Anyway, Michelle is too level-headed.'

'Michelle Dean is a child you should be very careful with,' Sally Baker told him. 'You hardly know her, but I do. She's secretive – that comes from Veronica of course – she's devious and I wouldn't put anything past her.'

Maltravers picked up the cup and sipped his coffee. Having decided to talk to Sally Baker because she was intelligent, he could not simply dismiss what she said as ridiculous.

'All right,' he agreed. 'Somebody left those things under the Lazarus Tree and I haven't got an immediate alternative explanation to what you're suggesting. First of all, is it Michelle?'

Sally Baker looked surprised at the question. 'Isn't it a reasonable assumption? Stephen says she's been hanging around the churchyard and you found her there yourself. But who put her up to it? And why?'

Maltravers indicated the book. 'Who else has this edition?'

'I only know of three other copies. Bernard Quex has one, there's another in the reference section of Exeter Library and the third belongs to an old couple who live over on the far side of the village. They're almost recluses. There may be others of course.'

'Michelle could have read the library copy for herself,' Maltravers remarked.

'Possibly, but she isn't the type to use the reference department, and even if she did why should she pick up that particular book?'

'Someone may have told her about it . . . but the end result's the same of course. Whoever drew it to her attention was manipulating her. So who is it – and why is she listening to them? Putting aside the stupidity of what she could be playing at, who's she trying to raise from the dead? Did she have some boyfriend who wiped himself out on a motorbike or anything like that?'

'Not as far as I know. There always seem to be plenty of boys about, but the ones her own age bore her. That's common enough. I've often thought that the male teachers at her school should tread very carefully if they don't want to make fools of themselves.'

'An older man then?' Maltravers suggested. 'Stephen might know if anything's going on at school.'

'What about Patrick Gabriel?' Sally Baker asked bluntly. 'Or do you want to keep stepping around that?'

Maltravers wondered how much he had been doing that, thrusting it from his mind because he found the idea distasteful. Gabriel's sex drive had been like an addiction with a predilection for young bodies; his talking openly about it had made it even more obscene. The availability of willing, cynically enthusiastic, street-smart girls in London had not excused his behaviour, but such girls went in with knowing eyes wide open and could look after themselves; a village teenager would be hopelessly vulnerable. Obsessed with dreams of city life, impressed with Gabriel's fame, naïve while deluding herself she was experienced, Michelle would have leapt at the excitement of it. And Gabriel would have casually used her, indifferent to any harm he was doing.

'She'd have been only about fourteen when Gabriel was here,' he said.

'Yes, she would. Sick, isn't it?' Sally Baker leant forward in her chair. 'I've got nothing specific to go on, but I met Gabriel

53

a few times in the Raven and he was obviously a lecher. Michelle hangs around the village in the evening and I saw him talking to her more than once. I can't imagine they were discussing poetry all the time. Stephen told me she was distressed when he died . . . and now I think somebody is trying to conjure up the dead. I don't like it, but it fits together.'

It did in a grotesque sort of way, but Maltravers wanted to knock it down. 'But there's no way I can see Michelle believing in Ralph the Talespinner. Anyway, it's only guesswork. There's no proof it's her.'

Sally Baker's eyebrows raised. 'Oh yes, there is. You gave it to me.'

'I did? How?' he demanded.

She looked wryly amused by the reaction in his face. 'Oh, you poor city innocent. You really can't see it, can you?'

'Can't see what?'

She sighed like a teacher losing patience with a slow pupil. 'Tell me again what you heard Michelle saying during the night.'

Still bewildered, Maltravers took out his diary. 'I could only hear parts of it . . .'

'Just the last bit.'

He checked what he had written. 'You mean, "born is that man"?'

'Exactly. One of the oldest tricks of witchcraft was saying the Lord's Prayer backwards. An ultimate blasphemy. Think about it.'

'So it's "Man that is born . . ."' Maltravers hesitated for a moment, then picked it up. '". . . of a woman hath but a short time to live and is full of misery".' As he looked at Sally Baker again, he felt suddenly chilled. 'From the service for the burial of the dead.'

'Precisely. And said in reverse to undo it. There's nothing about Mary Twelvetrees trying that in Ralph's story, but Michelle could have decided to add something herself – or been told to. Incidentally, what time did you hear her saying this?'

'I'm not sure . . . oh, yes. When I turned the light on, I noticed it was nearly half past midnight.'

'Patrick Gabriel's body was found at half past six in the morning and the police said he'd been dead for about six hours.' Her face defied further argument. 'Michelle Dean put those things under the tree. Don't try and tell me otherwise.'

Maltravers looked again at his notes, incomprehensible until Sally Baker had produced an explanation. Passing Michelle's bedroom door that morning, he'd glanced inside. Posters of New Kids on the Block and George Michael, clothes scattered on the floor, a ghetto blaster, books and coloured pencils on a desk unit, even soft toys on the unmade bed, survivors from childhood. All the normal images of modern adolescence – and mute witnesses to practices from old and dark superstition?

'For God's sake, she's just playing games.' He looked at Sally Baker as though seeking assurance. 'Isn't she?'

'Of course she is,' she agreed. 'But dangerous games – and we've now got reason to think they're somehow tied up with a murder.'

'So what do we do?'

'That's what we need to talk about.' Sally Baker smiled at him. 'Frankly, I'm awfully glad you've turned up. I've been worried about this, but Patrick Gabriel was almost certainly murdered by someone from this village and nobody knows who or why. So who could I approach about what I suspected was happening? How could I be certain I'd be safe?'

'There are surely some people you can rule out as the killer,' Maltravers argued. 'Some of them must have had alibis.'

'Not many when you get down to it. A few people were away, but of those who were here, being in bed, even with your wife or husband, in the small hours of the morning is easy to say and difficult to prove. The bottom line is that I could not be absolutely certain that whoever I talked to didn't know something about Patrick Gabriel's death. Asking questions could be dangerous.'

'But what about Stephen and Veronica?' Maltravers began, then hesitated uncertainly. 'I was about to say you had an obligation to talk to them – but if you were really worried that anybody you spoke to might be the killer, then that had to include them.'

'I'm afraid it did,' she replied. 'That was part of the problem.

55

I'm sorry, it's a horrible thing to say to you about your friends, but . . .'

'Don't apologise,' Maltravers interrupted. 'I can't bring myself to believe it, but I'm grateful to you for being so honest and I'll take it on board. Anyway, the immediate point is that you didn't talk to them about what you suspected Michelle might be up to.'

'Apart from being ultra-careful, I had no reason to.' Her hands made a gesture of frustration. 'All right, I thought that Michelle could be mixed up in it, but it's only now that you've provided me with some proof. What you have to remember is that after the murder, nobody in Medmelton knew how to play it. We tried to persuade ourselves it had been an outsider, but none of us really believed that. We were all suspicious and all under suspicion. I don't like thinking that way about people I've known for years, but life in the diplomatic service taught me to be very cautious. I've kept my thoughts to myself.'

'Including who the murderer might be?'

'No,' she corrected. 'Because I have no idea. Oh, I heard plenty of rumours, but they were nearly all based on settling old scores. Somebody had had a row with somebody else, so they took a perverted delight in hinting that there was something there the police ought to look into. They never went to the police with it of course, it was just malicious. Anyway, it was much better to persuade myself I was being hyper-imaginative. Harmless children's games under the Lazarus Tree was a much more comfortable explanation. Unfortunately, I can't bring myself to believe that now.'

She finished her coffee. 'So welcome to Medmelton, where women have strange eyes, people protect murderers from the police and witchcraft is still practised. It must make London seem quite safe.'

Chapter Six

Bernard Quex suffered from having enjoyed a childhood so happy that he had never wanted it to end. Up until their deaths in his forties, he continued to call his parents Mummy and Daddy, clinging to names that held warmth and security. Family holidays in the West Country had been a special bliss: the excitement of the drive from Sussex, the reassuring familiarity of the cottage they rented each year, the unchanging pattern of existence of the people who lived there, the rediscovery of remembered landscapes. When, eight years after his ordination, he had been offered the living of Medmelton, he had unquestioningly taken it as a sign that life had prepared him for such a place, to understand and protect it from change. For years, nothing disturbed that conviction as the villagers accepted him and he became one of them. Without realising it – without thinking about it – he abandoned a sense of vocation for mundane church activities, polite coffee mornings and the fellowship of the Raven. In a hollow of his beloved Devon hills, he had status, respect and, he persuaded himself, affection. A demanding sense of faith had been replaced by platitudes, a lost concept of calling by hospitable niceties. His congregation was obedient and undemanding, the parochial church council malleable, his bishop at a safe distance and God reduced to a lord-of-the-manor figure, Quex's benign social superior in an untroubled and comfortable world.

The one disaster had been Celia's death after only seven years of marriage. Losing the baby had denied her a desperately needed reason to live which she had not been able to find as his wife. Quex had never understood why she could not accept her share of his contentment. She had said such dreadful things about people in the parish, had been resentful of her duties, hated the social events and religious festivals, regular and dependable as the slow seasons. The more settled he became, the more her fretfulness grew until every day brought another crisis. Time and again he had tried to persuade her of what they had, of how important it was; but it had been important only to him. Separation was as unthinkable as divorce. When she suggested it, he would quote their marriage vows, citing the laws of the Anglican church in place of understanding, not so much because he was unable to understand but because he really did not want to. One afternoon he had returned from a christening to find her dead with the empty bottle of pills and had destroyed the note before calling the police. It was a truth not to be faced and he had later rationalised it to the degree where he actually believed the verdict of accidental death. If he accepted that Celia had been driven to taking her life, it meant there was something very wrong with his. And that threatened the security of a little boy racing across holiday meadows, laughing with happiness. So he had lied, persuaded himself he had not lied, and had been protected by the warm, unsuspecting sympathy of his parishioners. Celia was dead, but Medmelton still offered sanctuary.

Then evil had invaded his safe world. Patrick Gabriel had brought corruption, disturbing order, shaking the certainties that Quex needed. For a period, he had felt besieged, battling against an enemy who had penetrated his private fortress. At first he had reasoned that Gabriel would not stay long and could do no lasting damage, but then he had come to see him as a malignant virus that had to be destroyed before infection spread beyond hope of recovery. And the virus had been destroyed, almost literally cut out in a painful, bloody but necessary operation; the horror of violent murder had been eased by a sense of cleansing. The police investigation had passed, the wounds had begun to heal, normality had returned. Quex had regarded the villagers' reluctance to co-operate with the police as recognition that they also valued the sanctity of Medmelton's precious little world; not revealing the murderer had been a form of damage limitation and the pattern of bland sermons, safety and *goodness* had been restored. But he had started avoiding the Lazarus Tree, taking the long way round the churchyard from the lychgate to reach the rectory. Greeting worshippers in the west porch after Sunday services, he would not look at the sweet chestnut less than thirty feet away, laying silent siege to a life built on the deception both of others and of himself.

Then, like some malevolent force of nature, the tree had become the focal point of a revived evil and the tacit, unquestioned pattern that wove together church and everyday life was threatened again. Quex regretted he had ever told anyone about the things he had discovered in the churchyard, realising too late they were as corrupt as Gabriel's mutilated body. But he had impressed upon people that they were harmless and should be ignored. The majority had accepted his assurances – perhaps because they also wanted to – and those who had reservations had at least not done anything. But Quex knew how the fragile defences could crumble and now another stranger had arrived, one without an unquestioning love for Medmelton . . . and one who had known Patrick Gabriel. His conversation with Maltravers had been very brief, but the murder had been raised, perhaps out of passing curiosity, possibly for more dangerous motives. What could the man do? Nothing. He might talk to people, but they would tell him little if anything. In a few days he would leave, having learnt it was none of his business. Bernard Quex would continue to keep Medmelton safe, and in doing so would also protect his own reason for existence. As he walked through the village, dropping off leaflets for a church jumble sale, there were constant little encounters to remind him of what a benign God had placed in his care.

'Good morning, Mrs Tucker. Family well? Splendid . . . Oh, John, glad to catch you at home. The boiler's playing up again. Can you have a look at it? Thank you . . . And why aren't you at school, William? Sore throat? What sort of excuse is that? Make sure you're better for choir practice . . . Miss Gregg. How very kind of you to send that cake round to the rectory. Absolutely delicious. Your sister's well? Good . . . Dorothy, I meant to say on Sunday how wonderful the flowers looked. Tell David I want to know his gardening secrets . . . Good morning, Brigadier. Tackled *The Times* crossword yet? It's a stinker.'

How dare Patrick Gabriel have infested this sanctuary? He might have been a poet, but he had also been loud-mouthed and uncouth, an outsider contaminating good people. His ever-open pocket had made him popular in the Raven, but Quex had found him distasteful, telling obscene stories about his personal life in London even when there had been women at the bar. One night he had called Quex a hypocrite preaching a discredited and irrelevant God. Voice slurring with drink, his accusations had become increasingly outrageous, and what had appalled the rector was that nobody had tried to stop him; he even felt that in some ways many of them silently agreed. So Gabriel's death had been . . . no, it was sinful to call it divine punishment. It had been . . . appropriate, as though a malignancy had been removed. But did some poison remain, breaking out beneath the Lazarus Tree? As he returned to the rectory, Quex again avoided passing the tree and its sense of waiting terror.

Maltravers walked back to Medmelton from Sally Baker's. October had begun with autumn decay lit by sunshine fit for May, a wash of gold over browns, purples and fire oranges. Halfway down the hill he stopped and looked at a view that could have been lifted straight on to a Devon country calendar. He should be enjoying the pleasure of escape from London, not embroiled with an unknown killer and a girl playing some absurd game of what she thought was witchcraft when she was obviously intelligent enough to know better. What was Michelle really up to? Whoever was manipulating her might not be as much in control as they thought. If he – or she – could be found . . . but it apparently had to be someone with access to a first edition of Ralph the Talespinner. Anyone could have read the copy in Exeter Library and it would be impossible to trace them – which left some hermit couple . . . or the rector. For a member of the parochial church council, Sally Baker had been curiously ambivalent when Maltravers had mentioned the rector, softening his implication by suggesting he could have lent his copy to somebody.

'Perhaps,' she had agreed. 'But . . . oh, how can I put this? Bernard's slightly creepy sometimes. There's so much *goodness* about him that you begin to suspect it.'

'Clerics are meant to be good,' Maltravers had commented.

'Of course they are, but when they make you feel uncomfortable . . .' She had shrugged uncertainly. 'It's difficult to explain, but I don't really trust him sometimes.'

She could not – or would not – be more specific, but had suggested that he should speak further with Quex and draw his own conclusions. It was a fairly preposterous starting point, but there was nothing else to go on. Maltravers was disinclined to talk to Stephen again until or unless he had something specific to discuss; he was too close to the situation to be objective.

Immediately behind St Leonard's, with its own gate in the churchyard wall, the rectory had the appearance of late Victorian gentility reduced to distressed circumstances. Its net curtains needed washing and the brass step outside the front door was blotched dark brown verging on black; the entire house gave the indefinable impression of being in need of dusting. A weather-stained postcard pinned beneath the bell announced that it was not working, so Maltravers used the knocker. From somewhere inside a voice shouted, 'It's open!' and he pushed the door then stepped over the threshold. As he hesitated in the hallway, Quex called out again. 'In the study.'

The voice came from a room halfway down the hall and Maltravers went and stood in the open doorway. Quex was sitting at a desk in the alcove of a bay window with his back to him, writing.

'Won't be a moment, darling.' He spoke without looking round. 'I must just finish this list of helpers for the stalls before I forget who's doing what, then I'll be with you. You're earlier than I . . .'

'Hello again.' Maltravers felt he ought to say something before there were any more indiscretions. Quex whirled round, startled. 'Sorry to just walk in like this, but you did say that the door was open.'

'Yes. Of course. I . . .' The rector looked like a child rapidly thinking up an excuse when caught stealing. 'I was miles away. I hardly knew what I was saying. I'm sorry.'

'I'm the one who should apologise. I should have called out who I was. I'm afraid I'm interrupting you.'

'It's nothing important.' Quex turned away, somewhat unnecessarily, to close the notebook in which he had been writing. He stood up. 'How can I help you?'

'I want to ask a favour,' Maltravers replied. 'Stephen was telling me last night about Ralph the Talespinner and I said I'd like to read him. I understand you have a copy of his works and I wondered if I could possibly borrow it.'

'Ralph the Talespinner?' Quex sounded surprised. 'Doesn't Stephen have a copy?'

'He couldn't lay his hands on it . . . and anyway it's the later edition which I understand isn't complete. Yours is the original, isn't it?'

'Yes, I think it's . . . I'm not sure where mine is either. It's years since I read it. I'll see if I can find it.'

'Yes. But don't go to any trouble. I can always drive to Exeter and look at the copy in the library.'

Quex looked at him inquiringly. 'Why are you so interested? Nobody's ever classed Ralph as any sort of local genius.'

'I'm not expecting much,' Maltravers replied. 'But English literature is something of a passion with me, even when it's second division.'

'He doesn't qualify as literature at any level.' Now Quex sounded dismissive. 'If you want to read about this area of Devon, I can recommend . . .'

'You sound as though you're trying to put me off,' Maltravers interrupted. 'Are they really that bad?'

'They're . . . they're simplistic. They have a certain curiosity value, I suppose, but no merit otherwise. Believe me.'

Maltravers wondered if it was because his suspicions were heightened that he felt Quex wanted to be believed.

'I'd still like to read them, if you can find your copy,' he said. 'From what I've been told, Ralph seems to have had a vivid imagination.'

'Too vivid sometimes. I often wonder what effect he had on the people he told them to. He played on their superstitions.'

'Well, I don't think they'll have much effect on me – nor even on people in Medmelton these days.' The calculated remark went home.

'People who live in the country are as sophisticated as anyone else Mr Maltravers,' Quex said stiffly. 'And they resent being patronised.'

'I didn't mean to be patronising,' Maltravers replied levelly. 'I'm sorry if it sounded like that. Anyway, if you do find the book, I'll . . .'

'As I told you, I haven't any idea where it might be.' This was no longer the amiable rector making small talk with a visitor. 'However, if I do chance to come across it, I'll pass it on.'

As they were speaking, Quex had moved forward and Maltravers was still no further into the room than a couple of paces past the doorway. He was implicitly being asked to leave, and decided it would be best to do so when he heard the front door opening again.

'Bernard! It's me! Where are . . . ?'

Quex's eyes flashed past Maltravers and he instantly cut off the excited, too-happy voice. 'I've got a visitor in the study.'

'Oh.'

Maltravers reflected that a surprising amount could be injected into one unguarded syllable. Surprise, caution, acknowledgement of warning. He turned and looked down the hall. 'Hello again. I hope the coq au vin turned out all right.'

'What? Oh . . . yes. Thank you.' Ursula Dean was making as rapid an adjustment of her behaviour as Quex had done a few moments earlier. 'It was fine. I . . . I didn't realise anyone was here.'

'Mrs Dean's just come to help sort out a jumble sale,' Quex put in.

'I imagine they take a lot of organising,' Maltravers commented. 'I must let you get on with it. Sorry to have interrupted.'

Ursula Dean smiled nervously and stepped to one side as he walked towards the front door. She lowered her head as he passed, but he had already seen the carefully applied make-up and noted the high-heeled shoes and well-cut linen suit. She was excessively overdressed for a discussion about who would run the bric-à-brac stall and bore little resemblance to the woman he had seen panicking over her husband's dinner the night before.

'See you again,' he said and was through the still open door before he heard her make any response.

'Yes. Of course . . . goodbye.'

He had not gone five paces when he heard the door slam behind him and was somehow certain that Quex had closed it. He went out of the rectory gate opposite the back of St Leonard's and walked round to the west door. Beneath a ragged crown of dying leaves, sweet chestnuts were scattered beneath the Lazarus Tree, fruit gleaming brown and plump through splits in pale green coats of soft-spiked shells. He picked one up and peeled back the covering, the nut's surface slightly oily between his fingers. Perhaps there wasn't an affair going on — and perhaps it didn't rain in Indianapolis in the summertime. As neither Quex nor Ursula Dean appeared to have any skill at deception, they would give themselves away sooner or later, but people's private lives were not his business and he could see no immediate connection with what else was going on in Medmelton. More interesting had been Quex's obvious desire to put him off reading Ralph the Talespinner, strong enough to override his anxiety that Ursula Dean would arrive at any moment. Maltravers wondered if it really was years since the rector had read those stories.

Ursula Dean's palms were damp as panic pumped through her, escaping in hasty, shallow breathing and agitated heartbeats. She felt dizzy and sat down abruptly on a chair in the hall. As Quex turned from shutting the front door, she looked at him, seeking reassurance.

'Stephen told him about Ralph the Talespinner's stories but couldn't find his copy and he asked to borrow mine,' he said. 'That's all.'

'But he saw me here!' she protested. 'What will he think?'

'Nothing. You heard what I said about the jumble sale.'

'But did he believe it?'

'Why shouldn't he?' Quex took both her hands in his own. 'You're shaking, darling. Stop it. It's all right.'

'I'm scared.'

He pulled her to her feet and put his arms round her, smothering her trembling. 'Then don't be. Even if he thinks . . . no, he won't think anything. It's nothing to do with him.'

He placed his hands on her shoulders and held her away from him. 'It's nothing to do with anyone except us. I've already told you that.'

Ursula Dean pressed her head against him. The moments of ecstasy were brief, the hours of remorse endless. The memory of Bernard in silver and gold cape, hand raised to bless her marriage to Ewan, returned time and again to accuse her. Stories she heard and read about relationships such as they now had, casually begun and ended, never contained her sense of confused guilt. Dear God, what would her mother say if she ever found out? It was an affair between a man and a woman still essentially children, excited by the thrill of forbidden grown-up games but constantly terrified by them.

And Bernard Quex now had an additional concern. Maltravers had raised Gabriel's murder when they had first met that morning, perhaps only in passing, but . . . now he was specifically looking for a copy of a first edition of Ralph the Talespinner. Did he know something? If he did, what was it? And who else might have been talking to Stephen Hart's suddenly disturbing visitor? Had the virus returned in another form?

Maltravers had to wait to be served in Medmelton Stores where he had gone to buy flowers for Veronica; there were several people before him and each transaction involved a leisurely exchange of news and gossip. Every inch of space in the tiny shop was crammed with goods, piled, stacked and shelved in chaotic order. Bunches of dried herbs and strings of garlic hung from the ceiling amid soft toys in cellophane bags, canned fruit stood next to packets of washing powder, aftershave and cough mixture shared limited space with assorted boxes of screws and washers. A route complex as a maze wove round the floor past a march of silver steel shovels, a barrel of dried peas, sacks of smokeless fuel, a tower of yellow plastic buckets, folded deck-chairs and coiled green hosepipes. Next to the cold cabinet, wooden boxes were filled with vegetables mottled with rust-brown soil. Less than a square yard of counter was clear to serve customers, tightly hedged in by display stands of sweets, combs, tights, seeds, instant soup and packets of needles and crisps. You could buy scent, beer, wine, tinned lobster bisque, mops, electric fuses, firelighters, frozen Chinese meals, candles, stamps, children's clothes, a local paper or softback romantic fiction. It was sub-Post Office, supermarket, hardware store, clothes shop, newsagent's and chemist's packed into one room. And a do-it-yourself shop. And a baker's. And an off-licence. And a florist's. Maltravers felt that if he asked for a house-trained elephant he'd be offered a choice of Indian or African.

Shapeless body in a wrapover Paisley-pattern apron and grizzled hair harsh as steel wool, Mildred Thomson was clearly in her element, a focal point of village life, endlessly chatting as she sliced and wrapped cold meat, spun corners of paper bags into twisted ears or reached towards shelves without having to look where things were. She hardly stopped talking, but as each order, however complex, was completed, she knew the total price to the penny. When Maltravers reached the front of the queue, she took the two bunches of carnations, lilies, spider chrysanthemums and gypsophila, produced a large sheet of paper from beneath the counter like a conjurer and whipped them into a cone.

'Seven pounds,' she said, handing them back. 'You came in yesterday evening with Stephen Hart, didn't you?'

'That's right. I'm staying with him and Veronica for a few days.'

A bell tinged as the drawer of an ancient wooden till shot forward, a ten-pound note was flicked beneath a metal spring clip and three pounds change almost simultaneously extracted.

'Been to Medmelton before?' she asked.

'No.' Maltravers realised that even strangers were allotted their portion of conversation and he was expected to make his contribution. 'It's a beautiful village. You've always lived here, haven't you?'

'Apart from the war when I was in Plymouth.'

'It must have been quite a contrast living through the bombing,' he commented. 'Nothing as dramatic as that here.'

'Oh, you'd be surprised how much happens . . . we even had a murder once.' Liver-brown eyes sharpened, anticipating a reaction.

'I know. As a matter of fact, I knew him. Patrick Gabriel.'

'Oh.' She seemed disappointed at not creating some sort of sensation. 'Friend of yours, was he?'

'Not what you'd call a friend, but I met him a few times.'

'Is that why you're here? Because of him?' Extracting information to add to an extensive collection for passing on to others was an instinct with Mildred. Maltravers made an instant decision.

'In a way. To be perfectly honest, I didn't like him, but that doesn't mean that I think anyone should have killed him.' He registered that customers waiting to be served had abruptly stopped talking. 'From what I've found out, it looks as if the murderer must have been someone who lives in Medmelton.'

The 'found out' had an instant effect and Maltravers could sense sharpened ears behind him as clearly as he could see sudden suspicion in Mildred Thomson's face.

'The police didn't find anyone,' she said guardedly.

'Perhaps they didn't look in the right place.' Maltravers smiled disarmingly. 'Anyway, thank you for the flowers. Good morning.'

He turned to see four alarmed faces and the atmosphere was thick with unanswered questions as he walked out. He deliberately paused outside the door, forcing them to wait in frustration before they dared erupt into excited comment. Broadcasting it full volume from a loudspeaker in the middle of the village green could have been no more effective; virtually everyone would soon know that a stranger from London was staying at Dymlight Cottage and was making Patrick Gabriel's murder – Medmelton's very private affair – his business.

Chapter Seven

Nine miniature trophies won at the Medmelton and District Horticultural Show lined Alexander Kerr's mantelpiece, one less than the number of years since he had retired to the village. It had taken the first twelve months to prepare the earth before flawless onions, leeks for the Welsh to worship and cabbages that it was sacrilege to boil had begun to appear. How it was achieved remained unknown – as did a great deal more about him. It would have been foolish to let others know his growing techniques; it was contrary to the Official Secrets Act to admit what his job had been. Sally Baker, who had first met the mannered, pedantic, middle-grade cultural attaché at the British Embassy in Budapest, was one of fewer than twenty people in the world who knew at least part of it, and nobody knew it all. Kerr's CBE – which he never used – was a deliberately low-key official acknowledgement of a man whose subtle manipulation of shadowy contacts almost certainly saved John Kennedy's life for another year when he stood and looked across the Berlin Wall at the Brandenburg Gate in 1962, and once played a critical part in preventing Soviet tanks from crossing the Rhine. Even now, when the perilous Cold War world in which he had lived had gone, he occasionally went to London to give his opinions in what was unofficially called the Past Masters' Lecture Theatre in the Ministry of Defence basement. But such invitations were becoming infrequent and Kerr remained an anonymous retired civil servant with a gift for growing prize-winning vegetables who supplemented his pension as a part-time tutor in Romano-British history at Exeter University; it would have been indiscreet – in fact it was strictly forbidden – for him to offer lessons in any of the seven European languages in which he was fluent.

On Monday morning, he was translating *The Iliad* from the Greek into Polish (the impish fiction 'Translated by Peter Quince' appears in a surprising number of books) when the front doorbell rang. Neatly ordered papers and dictionaries disappeared into a desk drawer and the *Daily Telegraph*, crossword partly completed, was picked up as he went to answer it. Providing a covering explanation of what he had been doing had become part of his humour.

'Sally! If I'd known it was you, I needn't have bothered.'

'With what?'

'Masking the trail. Come in and tell me what the problem is.'

'Why should there be a problem?'

'Don't be obtuse, it doesn't become you,' Kerr replied as he led her through to the sitting room. 'It's Monday morning. You went to the stores as usual while the automatic washing machine was doing its business and it's a fine enough day to hang the things out. But I can see your garden from my window and the line is empty. Like anyone who was part of the diplomatic service, you're a creature of organisation, but today something's happened that's urgent enough to make you break the pattern. So you've not called round for an idle chat . . . do I really need to go on?'

She laughed. 'Oh, Alex, what an artist the world lost in you.'

'If you're going to quote, do it correctly,' he said sternly. 'This artist is not dead, but sleeping – with both eyes still open.'

'Then you can tell me what they've seen.'

Kerr's thin lips squeezed into a thoughtful moue at the tone of her voice. 'You sound . . . serious. Like you did when you first told me your suspicions about Bridgeman in the Prague visa office. And what a very nasty business that turned out to be. It cost two women's lives.'

'I try to forget about that,' Sally Baker said quietly. 'I knew one of them.'

'That's when I discovered how firmly you were anchored in our waters.' Kerr smiled comfortingly. 'Oh, dear. Wasn't that near the surface? I'm sorry I brought it up. Anyway, whatever this is, it surely can't be as painful.'

He guided her to a straight chair isolated in the middle of the room then sat opposite, hands folded together, sunlight filling the window behind him. Against the morning light, flint grey eyes were shadowed amid the web of lines — spun by years of deceit, plotting and strain — that covered his face like a net of pain. Instinctively, the innocuous gardening pensioner had put on the cloak of interrogator again.

'Relate,' he invited. 'From the beginning.'

'This isn't a Room 409 debriefing,' she reminded him. 'Stop letting old habits show. You shouldn't do that.'

'Sorry,' he apologised. 'But you're one of the few people with whom I can be myself again.'

'And who, pray, is that?' They smiled at each other before she continued. 'I'm going to start with this morning, because that's what has brought it all to the surface. Stephen Hart has a friend visiting him. He's called Augustus Maltravers.'

'The writer?' Kerr queried.

Sally Baker looked surprised. 'I don't know. Is he?'

'I can't believe there are two people with a name like that. His second novel came out about a year ago and he's written several plays. Nothing to trouble Iris Murdoch or Tom Stoppard, but better than a lot of the others.'

'It must be him, then. He's never said what he does — we've been too busy talking about other things. Anyway, now I will start at the beginning.'

Kerr listened for twenty minutes; although she could not see them, Sally Baker knew that the eyes were flickering occasionally as he mentally underlined key fragments of what his brain was simultaneously hearing and recording. When she finished, he would be able to write down everything she had said verbatim, including the hesitations which in the past had so often been crucial.

'Nothing more of immediate relevance or significance.' She smiled as she concluded. 'Now I'm back in 409.'

'And concise as ever,' he remarked. 'Action recommendation, if any?'

'Nothing by you, of course. But I'd like your thoughts. For a start, did you take any interest in Patrick Gabriel's death?'

'Naturally I reported it,' he replied. 'In my position, you don't ignore unexplained murders that close to the campfire. London sent a man down to talk to the police, but there wasn't a trace of anything. Gabriel's death was nothing more than a local mystery. I received a very comprehensive report – I think someone wanted to put the old boy's mind at rest. No especial suspects and a fair number were ruled out by the fingerprinting operation where they managed to do it.'

'Did you give your fingerprints?'

'Of course. I am ever the law-abiding citizen and I didn't want to draw the village bobby's attention to me. However, they were removed from the Exeter CID file within two hours.'

'So that's your interest taken care of. Any ideas on the subject?'

Kerr shrugged. 'Insofar as I gave it any thought, I felt the police concentrated too much on the motive for the murder rather than the motive for the theft. People murder for all sorts of reasons – the killer might just have been drunk, although I think that's unlikely – but stealing Gabriel's notebooks of poetry was much more intriguing.'

'But they had to be connected,' Sally Baker argued.

'Of course,' he agreed. 'But they put the cart before the horse – explain the murder and the theft will become clear. I'd have approached it from the opposite direction.'

'Did you put that to them?'

'Not directly, but when London gave the all-clear, I suggested they might pass it on as their idea. Not the sort of thing I wanted coming from me; shade too high profile. I don't know if London bothered.'

'And what about what's happening now? In the churchyard?'

'Guesswork and theorising.' Kerr lapsed dismissively into jargon. 'Blue sheet information only, pending confirmation from other sources. Coincidences with Ralph the Talespinner's story to be noted, but too many alternative possibilities for definite conclusions. Cannot at this stage be firmly linked to central event. No action unless . . .'

'Well I've taken action,' Sally Baker interrupted. 'Or at least I've suggested that Gus Maltravers does.'

'Then wait. Even totally inexperienced personnel can turn up data. Not likely to recognise it as such, but they report back and . . .'

'Oh, enough, Alex!' She glared at him crossly. 'This is Medmelton, not the Riga Corridor. And you've been retired for years.'

He laughed. 'You touch too many nerves. I tell myself it's a closed book, but my cover story becomes an old man's compensation. You walk in here with a mystery and I slip on the motley because I still miss wearing it. Forgive me?'

'Of course, and I understand. If I – or Gus – find out any more, can I talk to you again? Your thoughts might help.'

'Naturally. Bring your Mr Maltravers round. Tell him I'm a fan and would like to meet him; truth's always the best cover story. If nothing else, I can make an assessment of him.'

'We'll have to be careful.'

'He's hardly CIA,' Kerr pointed out. 'I've perfected the act and he'll just accept me as a pensioned-off member of Her Majesty's postal service. If I have any suggestions, I shall put them with garrulous hesitation and a suitable air of diffidence. You will treat me like a beloved antique and Mr Maltravers will be none the wiser.'

He paused for a moment. 'One final thing before you get back to the washing. What's your interest? Any . . . interface with Patrick Gabriel?'

'Not the slightest,' she replied emphatically. 'I met him . . . three times, four at most. I'm worried about Michelle Dean. Remember that I've come home and this is my village . . . perhaps I've become sentimental.'

'Yes.' Kerr sounded regretful. 'It's not an emotion I can afford to enjoy.'

If anything, Maltravers had underestimated the speed and efficiency of Medmelton's grapevine, although he could have anticipated its capacity for spinning theories of Byzantine complexity from the simple words 'found out'. By lunchtime thirty of Mildred Thomson's customers had been given the basic information, amplified with knowing glances and tacit hints, and had hurried away, clutching the news like a relay baton to be passed on as quickly as possible.

'He's police, of course. Been sent by London . . . Asked Mildred straight out if she knew anything. She didn't say anything of course, but . . . Drove off about ten minutes later. Harry says Special Branch use that make of car . . . He was in the Raven last night with Stephen Hart. Kept to themselves, talking. So what does Stephen Hart know? . . . Arrived yesterday, and – Peggy Travis saw this from her cottage opposite the church – went into the churchyard and was standing by the Lazarus Tree. She thinks he took photographs . . . Tall, thin, light blue eyes. Harris tweed sports jacket, cavalry twill slacks. Suede shoes. About forty. Touches of grey. Oh, no, he's not one of their hard men. Clever, though. Very polite. Good looking in a way . . . Stephanie was behind him in the stores. She reckons he was fishing . . . While he was in the pub, Sally Baker spoke to him. They obviously know each other. Might have met in London. It makes you wonder – and you know what her husband was of course . . . Went into the churchyard again this morning. Peggy says he wandered round behind the church and came back a few minutes later. He must have been looking at the cottage Patrick Gabriel rented. Empty at the moment. He's probably gone for a search warrant . . . Jim Henderson in the Raven says he was watching people at the bar. No one in particular, but you know who's always in there at that time of night, don't you? And Jim's certain he saw him in Exeter about a week ago . . . Listen. When he arrived – while he was in the churchyard, this was – Joy Drabble walked past his car and glanced inside. The way you do. There was a portable telephone on the seat. And an Ordnance Survey map. And a briefcase with one of those combination locks. Looked very official. And a pair of heavy walking shoes in the back. She didn't notice anything else. It was only a quick glance . . .'

By the time Maltravers returned in the afternoon, he could have created no greater buzz of excited interest than the arrival of a UFO. Conscious of the responsibilities of her key role in the matter, the conveniently situated Peggy Travis had been sitting by her front-room window for two hours, telephone by her side. She began to dial the moment his car turned by the church.

'I think there was somebody with him. Sitting in the back. Pardon? Oh, it would surely have been another man. But he drove past so quickly, I couldn't see properly. I'll watch for when they leave again. And Meg Williams was telling me that Ted says he definitely turned left at the main road this morning. He saw him from his tractor. So he could have been going to Plymouth. I once heard that Naval Intelligence has a secret place there. Do you think . . . ?'

Carrying a guide to Buckfast Abbey (obviously a rendezvous point to meet at least the head of Special Branch), Maltravers let himself in to an empty Dymlight Cottage and went through to the kitchen to make a cup of tea. Waiting for the jug kettle to boil, he glanced at the cork noticeboard fixed to one wall above the work surface. It carried the standard contents mixed with individual household touches: Michelle's homework time-table was pinned on the bottom of a picture of a tiger with the legend 'Go ahead – make my day'; an old newspaper cutting of events in Exeter with a concert by the Bournemouth Symphony Orchestra marked in ballpoint; recipes in Veronica's unreadable handwriting; paper clips in a plastic envelope with a label reading 'I live here – put me back!!'; money-off coupons and the menu from a Chinese takeaway; a formula for removing grease from clothing clipped out of a magazine; a cartoon of a middle-aged couple with the man saying, 'Remember when I had charisma and you had a flat?'; a photograph taken at some official dinner, Stephen self-conscious in a hired evening suit, Veronica out of focus.

And another photograph of – steam blossomed from the kettle and he poured water into a mug then returned to the board – a photograph of Michelle cross-legged on the floor of her room, looking up and pulling an instant face at the unexpected camera, open bedside cupboard behind her with . . . Maltravers took the picture down and stood under the kitchen light. Her shoulder hid the bottom of the cupboard, but the top shelf was partly revealed; a plastic doll was clearly visible, along with a small black book and something that looked like . . . he held the image closer and squinted but could not make out anything else. From the front room, he heard the granddaughter clock chime four; Stephen and Michelle would be home in about fifteen minutes, Veronica not until five o'clock. He put the photograph back and went upstairs. The bedside cupboard was locked and it would be hopeless searching for the key in a room that looked suitable for the attentions of the bomb squad. He returned to the kitchen and fished out the tea bag before taking the photograph down again and turning it over; written on the back was 'Caught by Stephen Hart, the phantom photographer, Michelle practises Buddhism and facial distortions to prove she really is fifteen today.' The proof that linked Michelle to the discoveries in the churchyard had been staring Stephen in the face for months.

Chapter Eight

Gilbert Flyte was agitated when he reached home on Monday
evening; part of the meticulous pattern which locked his life
together had been disturbed. Normally, he left the bank (by
long-standing arrangement with Mr Hood) at five twenty-one,
just ahead of the rush hour, and was back in Medmelton by
eleven minutes to six, in time to change, pour a medium sherry
and drink it with the tenth of his fourteen cigarettes a day while
watching the early evening news. Dinner with his mother and
Doreen began at six thirty, finished twenty minutes later and by
seven o'clock – no more than a minute either way – he was
ready to walk the dog, stop for two pints of beer in the Raven
and be back home by eight to work on his *Life of Nelson*, which
he had begun in 1986; after sixty thousand words, his hero had
still not joined the navy. Cocoa would be ready when he went
down to watch *News at Ten* when Mother went to bed and he
and Doreen followed her at a quarter to eleven. He read –
usually a thriller, sometimes a C. S. Forester Hornblower novel
again – and turned off the light at eleven fifteen. Each weekday,
the alarm clock went off at seven seventeen. Gilbert Flyte dressed
in the appropriate suit for the day (Monday olive green, Tuesday
dark blue, Wednesday the small check, Thursday the herring-
bone, Friday chocolate brown), listened to *Today* on Radio 4
while he ate breakfast (cornflakes from Easter to the end of
September; porridge the rest of the year), walked the dog over
an unalterable route and left for work at eight fifty-one, arriving
at the bank a precise nine minutes early to make up for the time
he left in the evening. So it had been throughout the fifteen years
he had been deputy manager, so it would ever be.

But on Monday, a delivery van blocking the side street which was part of his carefully plotted route had delayed him for a critical two minutes and forty-three seconds (he had timed it). Then he had been trapped behind a car transporter which meant the usual three minutes between the supermarket and the charity shop had taken an additional minute and a half. That meant the roundabout was thick with traffic when he reached it, adding another fifty-seven seconds before he could pull out. After that, it had been hopeless. Cars were pouring out of the factory gates when he reached them and two buses added to the congestion. It was nearly six o'clock before he reached the Medmelton turn – and of course Ted's tractor was on the lane. He arrived home at six eighteen, his life in ruins. As he pulled into the carport, Doreen appeared at the kitchen window, face tense with worry. During the previous twenty-nine minutes, she had convinced herself he must be dead; in her anxiety, she was half aware that the prospect brought a sense of horrified relief.

'Are you all right?' she asked as he walked in. Despite the cool of an October evening, a sheen of perspiration lacquered the bald head and the face that looked like one drawn by a child on a full moon. His tiny moustache, trimmed to millimetre precision, twitched. 'What happened?'

He told her everything; the name of the company that owned the delivery van, its make and colour and a detailed description of the driver, which town the car transporter had come from, precisely how many vehicles he had counted before he had been able to enter the roundabout, the numbers of both buses, exactly how far he had followed the tractor before reaching a passing space. In Gilbert Flyte's life, this had not been irritating inconvenience; this had been disaster. The evening was now impossible. There was no time for his sherry, he had missed the news and it was six thirty-nine before they sat down to eat. His mother made herself wait until they had all been served, then began to talk.

'I was in the stores this afternoon, and you'll never guess what Mildred says has happened.'

The impossible-to-answer question was followed by silence, inviting them to play their roles in the conversation. Already dismayed by the devastation of his life and the state of the steak and mushroom pie, Gilbert Flyte said nothing, so it was left to Doreen.

'What is it, Mother?'

'A man.' Vera Flyte loaded the announcement with significance and stopped again, ancient rabbit features trembling invitingly.

'What man?' Doreen asked obediently.

'From London.'

'From London?' Doreen was suitably impressed. 'Who is he?'

'Nobody knows.' She looked straight across the table at her son as she spoke, irritated that she could provoke no response.

'What's he doing here?' Such conversations happened all the time now and Doreen obediently played by the rules.

Her mother-in-law glared at Gilbert, defying him not to take an interest. 'Asking questions.'

'Questions about what, Mother?' Doreen was aware that this news had been carefully kept secret until her husband came home, but that was invariably the case.

Vera Flyte stretched the moment as far as she could by taking another mouthful of food and chewing it thoroughly before producing the first fat morsel of real drama. 'About the murder. Of that poet.'

'The murder?' Abruptly, Gilbert Flyte did respond. 'Who is he?'

'Well, after he went in the stores, Mildred was talking to . . .'

It took her more than ten minutes to recount the complete range of possibilities with her own additional observations and Doreen noticed that Gilbert stopped eating as he listened. Had he suddenly taken all his clothes off and started dancing on the table, it could have been no more incredible.

'. . . so, I reckon he's either a private detective or he's been sent by the Government. I think somebody somewhere knows something and he's here to investigate it. People would get suspicious – be on the qui vive – if they sent a policeman in uniform, so he's here pretending to be visiting Stephen and Veronica Hart.' Having said several things three or four times, even Vera Flyte could drag it out no further.

'Fancy.' Doreen spoke automatically to give her mother-in-law's story the proper level of respect, but was looking at her husband. 'Are you all right, Gilbert? Do you want one of your pills?'

'What?' Flyte shook himself. 'No. Of course not. Why should I?'

'You don't look too well. Are you sure that . . . ?'

He interrupted with a rattle of short, snapped-out sentences. 'It was the journey. Very upsetting. I'm all right. Nothing's the matter. Why should there be? Dinner late as well. Look at the time. Past seven.' He stood up, meal still unfinished. 'Where's Bobby? He wants his walk. Bobby? Bobby? Here, boy. Good dog. Come on, then.'

Stumpy tail wagging, the wire-haired terrier trotted from force of ingrained habit to the back door where his lead hung on a hook. Flyte clipped it to his collar and was gone.

'Gilbert's not had his pudding!' Vera Flyte's concern was not for her son's welfare. 'There is pudding, isn't there? On Monday, we have . . .'

'Yes, Mother. It's all right. I'll fetch it for you.' Doreen was looking across to the front window – even on the darkest nights, the curtains were never drawn until after their meal – watching her husband unlatch the garden gate and walk away in the gloom.

'Good.' Her mother-in-law's mind was put at rest. 'Treacle tart on Mondays. I like treacle tart. With a drop of cream tonight, please.'

'Cream,' Doreen repeated absently as she left the table. 'With the treacle tart. I'll just get it.'

At least the kitchen was normal, treacle tart ready cut on three dishes, tub of single cream in its correct place in the fridge. But she was shaking as she poured it, unable to cope with the disorientating events of the evening. Late home, everything thrown out of order, meal not completed, Gilbert's regular, boring, but oh-so-secure behaviour in chaos. And he had looked shocked when Mother started talking about this stranger who'd arrived in the village. This man with an interest in the murder everyone had forgotten about. Cream overflowed the edges of the shallow dish, another little twist of frightening confusion.

*

As Maltravers and Stephen entered the Raven, there was not exactly an instant silence but a distinct frisson of wary attention ran through the bar. Conversation paused then continued in lower voices and several pairs of eyes watched both men cautiously as they ordered drinks. Stephen did not appear to be immediately aware of the atmosphere, but Maltravers had been anticipating it. He had not mentioned either his discussion with Sally Baker or his provocative comments in Medmelton Stores, correctly reasoning that gossip about them would be carefully kept from reaching Dymlight Cottage.

'Where's Gilbert tonight?' Stephen asked as the landlord, Jim Henderson, served them.

'Not in yet.' Henderson glanced at the glass-fronted pendulum case clock on the wall. It was nineteen minutes past seven. 'Strange.'

'It's incredible,' Stephen corrected. 'What's happened?'

Henderson shrugged. 'Don't know. Excuse me.'

'Who's Gilbert?' Maltravers asked as the landlord turned away.

'What?' Stephen was watching Henderson in surprise. 'Oh, Gilbert Flyte. He's always here at ten past seven on the dot.'

'Always?'

'Never misses.' Stephen frowned. 'But Jim doesn't seem concerned.'

'Should he be?'

'He should be, but . . .' Stephen shook his head before explaining. 'Gilbert's a psychoneurotic obsessive. Classic case. Bolts the back door before going to bed, cleans his teeth, wonders if he did the door, goes down and checks, reads in bed, worries about the door again, back downstairs. It can go on half the night. His life's regulated down to the tiniest detail. He walks through that door at ten past seven, drinks two pints from his own personal tankard and leaves at six minutes to eight. They could set Greenwich by him.'

'What would make him late?' Maltravers asked.

'The end of the world.' Stephen looked at Henderson, now talking to another group of customers, then round the rest of the bar. He raised his voice. 'Where's Gilbert got to?'

Several people looked towards him, then someone said, 'He's late,' before they all turned away again.

'Nobody seems very bothered,' Maltravers commented quietly. 'Now who's getting neurotic?'

'Not me,' Stephen said firmly. 'They should be talking about nothing else.'

Maltravers gazed casually round the bar, noting heads close together like plotting revolutionaries, talk muted, backs forming secretive enclaves. He could only guess by how much Medmelton had inflated the significance of his presence, but it appeared to have been enough to drive everything else from the communal mind. As he wondered how they were going to deal with it, Henderson took on the role of tacitly elected spokesman. He gave a slight, almost conspiratorial, nod to the men he had been talking to, straightened up from where he had been leaning against the bar and came back, covering the manoeuvre by picking up a blue and white chequered linen cloth and starting to polish glasses from the shelf next to where Maltravers was sitting.

'Hear you're from London,' he said.

'That's right.' Maltravers nudged Stephen's leg with his foot, indicating he wanted him to stay quiet. 'Down for a visit.'

'Business as well?'

'You could call it that.' Now the bar had gone silent.

'What sort of business?'

'Personal.' Maltravers had spent the afternoon rehearsing responses to possible conversations, designing them to make anyone who might question him reveal the nature of their interest.

'Personal,' Henderson repeated. 'In Medmelton. Been here before?'

'No.' Maltravers smiled. 'Lovely village.'

'Thought I saw you in Exeter the other week.' Henderson held a glass up to the light, then looked back at Maltravers inquiringly.

'Not me. I was still in London.'

'You've got a double then.' Now Henderson sounded challenging, daring further denial.

'I must have.' As Maltravers refused to be goaded into what could be made into an argument, Henderson's silent audience was almost tangibly willing him to continue.

'Anything to do with the village, is it? Your business?'

'There could be a connection. I'll have to see.'

It was mildly offered minimal information that revealed nothing definite and showed that Maltravers was not to be drawn. Henderson appeared uncertain how he could press any further and gave up.

'Well, if there's anything you want to know about Medmelton, not much misses my ears.'

'Thank you. I'll bear that in mind . . . Can I buy you a drink?'

'I've already got one, thanks.'

Disappointment followed the landlord as he retreated to the other side of the bar and there could have been an uncomfortable silence if Gilbert Flyte had not arrived at that moment. People who had been uninterested in his absence minutes earlier were suddenly full of excited questions.

'What was that all about?' Stephen muttered.

'Tell you later,' Maltravers murmured back. 'Anyway, now that the ice has been broken, introduce me to a few people.'

The reception was near enough hostile to make no difference. Several offered only reluctant grunts of greeting and the best responses were little more than the most basic comments, spoken as though under police questioning. Storing away names and what little information accompanied them, Maltravers remained amiable, making the intelligent small talk of a harmless visitor, giving no indication of being offended. Gilbert Flyte was the only one who revealed any suggestion of positive apprehension at being approached.

'Gilbert, I'd like you to meet Gus Maltravers, a friend of mine from London.' Under normal circumstances, Stephen would have left Flyte out – any encounter with him inevitably led to conversations of mind-numbing tedium – but resistance everywhere else left him with no option. 'Gilbert's an assistant bank manager in Exeter. Lives in the cottage just along from here on the corner of the green.'

'Hello,' Maltravers hoped his smile was wearing well. 'I gather you were unexpectedly late this evening.'

'What?' Flyte appeared to be considering endless threatening motives behind the comment. 'Oh, yes. Got held up. Nuisance.' He turned to his dog. 'Stay, Bobby.' Immobile as a rock by his master's bar stool, the terrier looked confused.

'I noticed your cottage when I arrived,' Maltravers added. 'It looked very attractive at a distance. What is it? Eighteenth century?'

'Late. Seventeen nineties.' Flyte finished the remaining half of his pint in three hasty gulps and spluttered. 'Anyway, nice to meet you, Mr ... er ... Mr ... Mallory, but I have to go. Come on, Bobby.'

For the first time ever, Gilbert Flyte left the Raven eight minutes early. Already amazed at Maltravers not being subjected to a never-ending narrative either of his journey home or the detailed history of his cottage, Stephen Hart waited for the uproar that did not come. Knotted into separate groups again, nobody appeared even to notice.

'We ought to be getting back as well,' Maltravers said. 'Dinner will be ready.'

'Pardon?' Stephen looked blank. 'Yes, of course.'

Maltravers drank the last of his wine and put his glass down, nodding towards a man who happened to be looking in his direction.

'Goodnight,' he called loudly enough for everyone at the bar to hear. 'Probably see you tomorrow.'

Stephen controlled himself until they were twenty yards from the pub. 'What the hell is going on? What have you been up to?'

'Very little, but obviously enough,' Maltravers replied. 'I made a few casual comments to Mildred Thomson this morning and Medmelton has done the rest.'

'What sort of comments?'

'Just enough to suggest that I had more than a passing interest in Patrick Gabriel's death. I assumed the word would get around ... and I now don't seem to be a welcome stranger in the camp.' Maltravers looked back at the Raven. 'I'd love to be a fly on the wall in there at the moment.'

'What are you hoping to achieve?'

Maltravers shrugged. 'Flush somebody out of cover? Nobody's going to talk to me willingly, so the pond has to be stirred. I have mixed metaphors for all occasions. First concrete results are that one Gilbert Flyte appears strangely resistant to the pleasure of my company.'

'You don't know how unbelievable that was,' Stephen told him. 'Arriving late was one thing – all right, so he was held up – but him not telling you the story of his life and walking out early was like the sun rising in the west.'

'And all because you introduced him to me?'

'I can't think of any other reason.'

'Not a bad start,' Maltravers remarked. 'Tell me more about him. Out here. Let's keep this between just the two of us for the moment.'

There was a flash of sudden alarm in Stephen's glance. 'You mean you don't want Veronica to know?'

'Not yet. Don't get me wrong, I'm not suspecting her of anything. But she's very much a part of Medmelton and might not be . . . detached enough.'

'You mean in relation to Michelle?'

'You said that, not me,' Maltravers replied evenly. 'You've asked me to try and help and I'd appreciate it if you'd let me do it my way.'

'Are you keeping something from me?' Stephen asked.

'Frankly, yes,' Maltravers admitted. 'Because it's no more than a bizarre theory and I don't want you worrying unnecessarily. Trust me. If there are things you have to know, I'll tell you.'

Stephen stared at him closely, then accepted. 'All right. But don't keep me in the dark too long. Too many people are doing that.'

'You'll have chapter and verse when the time comes,' Maltravers promised. 'Now let's have the potted history of Gilbert Flyte, neurotic of this parish.'

'There isn't much to tell. He wasn't born in Medmelton, but has lived here for more than twenty years. Married, no children, mother lives with them. He could bore for the planet, but otherwise he's harmless.' Stephen paused. 'There's hardly anything else to say about him. Churchwarden, scorer for the village cricket team ... oh, and writing an endless biography of Nelson.'

'A Thoreau life of quiet desperation?' Maltravers suggested.

'He'd not see it like that. He's perfectly contented in his little rut. A lot of people are.' Stephen shrugged. 'But there could be other hang-ups below the surface. Still waters run deep.'

'Still waters stagnate,' Maltravers corrected. 'And nasty things breed in them. The fact is that your Mr Flyte starts acting completely out of character the moment he meets me.'

'So did everybody else,' Stephen pointed out. 'Medmelton may be insular, but if anyone local turns up at the Raven with a visitor people are friendly enough. They treated you as though you've got the plague.'

'Well, I have been ringing my leper's bell.' Maltravers looked back across the empty green to the pub, windows glowing crimson in the darkness. 'I must try ringing it again – a bit louder next time.'

As they walked on, Gilbert Flyte instinctively turned off his desk light as he saw them from his upstairs study, as though invisibility would protect him. He watched as they passed under a street lamp illuminating the ford, Maltravers making some gesture with his hand, Stephen walking with his head bowed. From nearly a hundred yards across the green, it was impossible to interpret anything from that momentary glimpse, but as they disappeared into the darkness and he turned the light back on, his fingers left a smear of sweat on the switch. Then he stared at St Leonard's churchyard and the dim outline of the Lazarus Tree for a long time as guilt and the terror of exposure with which he had lived for months returned to consume him again.

Chapter Nine

Behind the activity of Medmelton Stores with its changing stock and constant passage of people, the sitting room was a slow, quiet ruin of Mildred Thomson's childhood and her parents' lives; heavy oak dining suite and sideboard with yellowing linen runner, mahogany case clock in the centre, metal-bound wooden biscuit barrel and stuffed magpie, perched alert in death on a branch under a glass dome, at either end. The bulbous sofa was infested with dust, the Axminster time-worn as a medieval tapestry, the mantelpiece over the blacklead fireplace covered with ornaments from another age: a pair of Chinese dogs, a boy perpetually holding cherries above a rosebud mouth, a grim bronze bust of Gladstone, a George VI coronation mug. Behind decorative plates and faded imperial images – the death of Gordon and Indian tiger hunts – the wallpaper her father had hung thirty years earlier was still cream; what could be seen had darkened to dirty mustard. Old and musty as the room itself, Mildred was watching television when she heard the back kitchen doorlatch click; it was never locked until bedtime.

'Is that you, Michelle?' A remote control – one of few contemporary touches – killed scenes of sophisticated America and the screen became a blind eye. Mildred turned and looked over the humped back of the sofa as the girl appeared in the doorway. 'I'm glad you've come. I need to talk to you.'

Michelle rocked slightly on the wooden chair, sitting on a knitted patchwork cushion made by Mildred's mother limp from countless washings, original colours blurred into muddy pink and yellow. The room depressed her with its sluggish corruption and sense of maggot decay; but Mildred gave it the fascination of the repulsive, the thrill of a horror film.

'Who's this man visiting you?'

'What?' The immediate question caught the girl unawares. 'You mean Gus? He's a friend of Stephen's. Why?'

'He came into the shop this morning.'

'So?'

'He said he was investigating the murder.'

The girl looked startled. 'That's stupid. It's nothing to do with him.'

'He says it is . . . has he spoken to you?'

'A bit.' Michelle looked away at smokeless flames weaving like shadows of wild dancers in the grate. 'He's all right.'

'What did you talk about?'

'Not much . . . London – he lives there.'

'Did he mention Patrick?'

'No.' The girl looked back at Mildred. She had her toad face on, unblinking eyes, sagging flesh beneath her chin stretched as she held her head forward. Michelle began to feel defensively angry. Mildred didn't own her – nobody did – and if she wanted to talk to anyone about anything that was her business. 'What did he mean by investigating? He's not a policeman. I can tell you that. He's a writer. Stephen's known him for ages. Mum knows him as well.'

'He didn't say why he was investigating. Just that he was.'

Michelle suddenly remembered seeing Stephen and Maltravers near the Lazarus Tree shortly after his arrival – where he had later spoken to her. Had he been watching her? She tried to recall what had been said. He'd asked what she was doing in the churchyard, but had not pressed her. They'd talked about London and how she wanted to go there . . . and she'd mentioned Blackheath. The way her mind had been working at the time, it had been an almost inevitable question. If he was really investigating, surely he would have used that as an excuse to say something about Patrick. But he hadn't. What had he said? Ignored at the time because it wasn't important, it was now gone.

'You didn't tell him anything, did you?' she asked.

87

'Of course I didn't.' Mildred looked at her pityingly. 'I just wanted to warn you to be careful with him.'

'He's hardly taken any notice of me.' She could persuade herself that was true; one chance conversation didn't mean anything. 'Don't worry. He's only here for a few days.'

She dismissed Maltravers from the conversation; he was just another irrelevant grown-up in her life, vaguely interesting because he lived in London, but finally as boring as all the others.

'I want to talk about what I do next. I've done all the other things like you said.'

Mildred Thomson's smile showed crooked teeth and inflamed gums. This was the obedient Michelle Dean, feeding her need to be wanted by another human being, acknowledging qualities that made her unique.

'You're nearly there,' she said. 'Come on. We'll ask the glass. You lay everything out.'

Michelle took a pack of cards, creased with repeated use, from the sideboard drawer. There were all the letters of the alphabet, figures from zero to nine and two with the words 'Yes' and 'No'. Cracked backs bore a picture of a crystal ball filled with swirling smoke around a spectral, slightly menacing face. She laid them out in a precise circle on the polished dining table, the 'Yes' and 'No' cards opposite each other, then placed a glass tumbler upside down in the centre. Mildred eased her flabby body off the sofa and they sat opposite each other, forefingers of their right hands resting on the bottom of the glass.

'Wait,' Mildred warned as she saw the glitter of anticipation in Medmelton eyes. There was a silence broken only by a tumble of coal and the ticking of a clock on the sideboard. Michelle's eyes never left the glass as her expectation grew into tenseness.

'Is anybody there?' Mildred Thomson's voice was very low. For a few seconds nothing happened, then the glass began to slide towards 'Yes'. Michelle had deliberately placed the card in front of the old woman on the far side of the table. She was not pushing the tumbler and Mildred Thomson's finger was barely touching it.

'Who are you?'

The glass returned to the centre and stopped for a moment,

then began to pick out letters one at a time: 'P . . . A . . . T . . . R . . . I . . .'

'Is it Patrick?' Mildred interrupted. The glass diverted to 'Yes'. 'Did you find the flowers?'

'W . . . H . . . A . . . T . . . F . . . L . . . O . . . W . . . E . . . R . . . S?'

'Under the tree.'

The glass's movement to 'Yes' seemed hesitant, as if confused.

'They were for you.'

'W . . . H . . . Y?'

'Don't you know.'

'No' was directly in front of Michelle and her body jerked as the glass slid to it so quickly that it knocked the card slightly out of the line of the circle.

'Yes you do,' Mildred murmured soothingly.

Now back in the centre, the tumbler oscillated in tiny circles then stopped. Mildred breathed in and out very deeply.

'You speak to him,' she whispered.

Michelle had to swallow to clear her throat before she could speak. 'Are you all right?'

For half a minute nothing happened, then the glass suddenly whipped around the table. 'H . . . E . . . L . . . P.' Michelle went very pale as it returned to the centre and immediately repeated the word.

'It's all right, it's all right,' Mildred assured her hastily. 'Let him rest for a moment.'

The girl could hear her heart beating as they both waited. Once the glass seemed to try to move, and she could almost feel agitation, even a sense of pleading, emanating from it.

'Be at peace,' Mildred repeated softly. 'What is this girl called?'

When it had first happened, this had been the most chilling moment and even now Michelle felt a sense of terrified wonder as her name was obediently picked out letter by letter.

'And she is your friend, isn't she?' Mildred added. The movement to the 'Yes' card seemed very slow. 'And I am your friend.'

Michelle let out a tiny scream as the glass jumped beneath their fingers, cracking back on the table top and quivering violently. It skidded across the polished wood, first to 'No', then to 'Yes', then shot back to the centre where it moved rapidly from side to side before streaking out at a crazy sequence of letters. 'H . . . E . . . L . . . A . . . T . . . R . . . O . . . N . . . P . . . O . . . E . . . G . . . A . . . B . . . R . . .' The girl tried to pull her fingers away, but they seemed glued to the glass. She looked desperately at the old woman, whose features were twisted with what looked like fear or anger.

'What's happening?' Michelle cried. 'Stop it! Stop it!' She did not know if she was speaking to the glass or to Mildred. The tumbler was still hitting the cards violently, pushing them further and further towards the edge of the table until one fluttered on to the girl's lap. The finger of one hand still captured, she used her other hand to brush the card away in frantic revulsion, as though it was a spider. As she screamed, the glass shot away as though someone had thrown it, flying across the room and shattering against the wall. Mildred Thomson's body shuddered and the stillness was like phantom peace after a thunderclap.

'Wh . . . wh . . .' Michelle sobbed as she tried to speak. 'What happened?'

Mildred held up her hand, indicating she was still recovering. After a few moments, she nodded as though she had explained something to herself.

'It's this man. This visitor.'

'What do you mean?'

'He's an outsider and he's interfering. The vibrations are very bad.'

'But . . . but what's he *done*?'

'We don't know. That's the problem.' She glanced at the girl sharply. 'He's been seen in the churchyard, you know. I should have realised that would cause a disturbance. Have you seen him there?'

Unthinking admission came out of her terror. 'That's where I talked to him.'

'Then that's it! Why didn't you tell me before we started?' Mildred was suddenly accusing. 'Did you let something slip out?'

'Of course not. I'm not stupid.'

'You've got to be careful. I've told you that time and time again. He's only here for a few days, isn't he? Have as little to do with him as possible. Once he's gone, it will be all right.'

Michelle looked at the cards strewn across the table, mute reminders of desperate agitation. She had never been as scared in her life as during those endless seconds of insane violation. The room's mildewed sense of age now carried a chill of malevolence; the game had become nasty and the knowing adolescent was a frightened little girl. The thought of home was a promise of sanctuary.

'I've got to go. I said I'd be back by ten.'

Mildred Thomson did not move as the girl walked out. She heard the outer kitchen door close, then gathered the cards together in claw-bent fingers and tapped the pack on the table top. She would have to be cautious now if she was to keep her precious hold over Michelle Dean. She was also aware that she did not understand what had happened.

Out of compulsive habit, Gilbert Flyte had set out his notes and reference books in order before inserting the disc in his word processor and calling up 'Chapter Twenty: The Scent of the Sea'. But the regular and regimented had provided no retreat. Incapable of rationalisation, he could only worry, conjuring up increasingly threatening possibilities, each convincing him that it would become reality. Madcap imagination whipped tiny details into tidal waves of panic. The first thing the man . . . what the devil was his name? . . . had asked was about the cottage. What did he suspect? What did he *know*? Had he been spying? Asking questions? Who had sent him? Each theory his mother had produced at dinner seemed plausible until Maltravers assumed the proportions of every authority figure in the world; and Gilbert Flyte held such people in excessive and fearful respect.

He tried to force himself to be calm. There had never been the slightest suggestion of anyone suspecting anything. While he had at first tried to find the courage to defy the police, he had of course let them take his fingerprints and nothing had happened – which meant they were satisfied. Or did it? Had they gathered some evidence together and were looking for the rest? There had been strangers in Medmelton during the summer, not many and they had been ignored as tourists, but tourists hardly ever came. One man had taken photographs in the churchyard . . . and at that cricket match when Flyte had been scoring. Had he taken a picture of him, passing it off as a holiday snapshot when it was actually for an official file?

Like new outbreaks of flame in a forest fire, fresh worries flared in his mind. How long had this man been here? Had he already talked to Doreen – she'd chat to anybody – probing with subtle skill, extracting more fragments of information? Had he met Mother when she was wandering round the village? She was worse than Doreen, telling complete strangers the entire family history. He probably carried a hidden tape recorder, now filled with unguarded comments to be analysed against what the police already knew as they relentlessly built up their case. And tonight in the Raven, he had made his approach seem so casual – they were trained to do that of course – as he began to close in. The little finger of Gilbert Flyte's right hand began to twitch . . . he jumped violently as there was a hesitant knock on the study door.

'What is it?' Accumulated panic burst out in his voice.

'Gilbert? Are you all right?' Through the door, Doreen sounded bewildered; nothing less than the house being on fire would have allowed her to open it. '*News at Ten* has started.'

'I'm not . . . I'm busy . . . I'll be down shortly.'

Conditioned by years of never entering the study while her husband was working in the evening, Doreen Flyte gave a little nervous whimper then went back downstairs. Gilbert's cocoa and two chocolate digestive biscuits were on the table by his chair, the newscaster had just completed the headlines and was starting the main story, everything was in its immutable place in the room. Sitting on the hearthrug, Bobby looked at her, mutely seeking an explanation for his master's absence. Doreen clung to her own routine for reassurance, clasping her hands round the comforting warmth of her mug of cocoa and staring at the screen; if they had announced the assassination of the entire royal family, she would not have registered what they were saying.

Familiar since childhood with life in the country, nights of silence and unbroken darkness had held no alarms for Michelle Dean. But when she escaped from Mildred Thomson, it was into the familiar become menace. Invisible goblin presences crouched all over the green she had to cross and the tower of St Leonard's, shadowed in clouded moonlight, waited like a hungry creature whose lair she had to pass. Tears of panic blurring her eyes, she ran through one terror towards another, the tower growing bigger and more dreadful as she approached it. She overcame a shrieking, insistent impulse to look towards the Lazarus Tree as she raced down the path alongside the churchyard wall, crying as she stumbled on a root, then dashing on to where Dymlight Cottage's high hedges promised protection. She burst through the front door as though devils howled at her heels.

'What the hell's the matter?' Stephen snapped with alarm as she crashed in, slamming the door behind her and leaning against it, panting. He was sitting in the wingback chair by the fireplace. Maltravers and her Uncle Ewan on the chaise-longue opposite him; all of them were looking at her. There was no sign of her mother. It was painful as she swallowed and heartbeats pounded through her head.

'I . . . I've been running,' she gasped. 'I'm late.'

'It's only five past,' Stephen said. 'We weren't worried.'

'Where's Mum?'

'She's just gone to bed. Bit of a headache . . . are you all right? You look as though . . .'

'Of course I'm all right.' Safe now, Michelle's self-confidence was beginning to return. It was childish to let adults know you were scared of anything. 'Hello, Uncle Ewan. How's Auntie Ursula?'

'She's fine.' Ewan Dean dismissed the conventional inquiry. 'Where've you been?'

'Just out. To see Ann and Frances . . . Can I finish these?' She crossed to where a couple of stuffed olives remained in a dish on an occasional table next to Maltravers. She had regained enough control to know that the best way of deflecting interrogation was to behave normally.

'Help yourself,' Maltravers said. Her uncle and stepfather seemed to be relaxing, persuaded there was no immediate crisis, but he still watched the girl closely. A terrified child had burst through the door, cloak of adolescent false courage in shreds. The previous evening she had returned home nearly an hour later, irritatedly impatient towards criticism and concern.

'Who are Ann and Frances?' he asked as she took the olives.

'What?' So bland a question should not have produced the apprehension that flashed across her face. 'Just girls from school. I often go and see them. They're twins . . . we're in the same class. We help each other with homework . . . then play records and that. Talk . . . we don't do anything silly, like . . . well like anything.'

She hated the way she could not stop offering explanations when none was needed. She suddenly realised how blue Maltravers's eyes were – like Patrick's, but lacking that metallic glint. She swallowed again and gagged on a half-chewed olive.

'I'll get some water,' she choked and ran to the kitchen. Maltravers watched her back as she stood at the stainless steel sink and noticed the spasm of agitation that shivered across her shoulders. He exchanged a concerned glance with Stephen, then picked up the conversation he had been having with Dean when they were interrupted. It seemed best to lay down natural cover for what he was certain would be Michelle's retreat to bed.

'Is there enough business in Exeter to support a specialist model shop?' he asked. 'Or do you do mail order as well?'

Dean began to explain the differences between serious and casual collectors, but Maltravers noticed that his eyes kept flicking towards the kitchen door and he broke off when Michelle came back.

'Better now?' he inquired.

'Fine. I'm going to bed. Goodnight.' Nervous loquaciousness when Maltravers had spoken to her had been replaced with minimal communication again. As she left the room, Dean appeared to have forgotten that he had been talking.

'Which are the most popular models?' Maltravers prompted.

'Pardon? Oh, it goes in cycles. After the Gulf war everybody wanted Tornados or the Stealth bomber. Some even asked if we did Scud missiles. Proper collectors are more consistent.' Michelle disappeared upstairs and Dean turned back to him. 'Are you interested?'

Maltravers laughed. 'Hardly. I'm hopeless at things like that. When I was a kid I tried building a model Spitfire out of a kit and it ended up about as aerodynamic as the British Museum.'

Stephen began telling his brother-in-law of how he had once found Maltravers helplessly surrounded by the wreckage of a toaster, having failed to establish at the outset that the fuse in the plug had blown, and of the time when . . . Long unapologetic for his practical incompetence, Maltravers had the sense that Dean's attention was somehow detached. After a few minutes, he glanced at his watch and said he had to go. The two men remained silent as they heard the kitchen door into the back garden close behind him.

'Well?' Stephen finally asked elliptically.

'I think the first thing to do is check with this Ann and Frances,' Maltravers replied. 'Obliquely of course. You'll see them at school tomorrow?'

'Yes, they're in my fourth-year set. Do you think she was with them tonight?'

'Frankly, no. And lying when it could be checked so easily was either stupidity or panic. But she's not stupid. The point is, where was she? And what was she doing?'

'God knows.' Stephen shook himself as though to break claws of unease. 'What the *hell* is happening, Gus? You said you knew something.'

Maltravers lit a cigarette. 'I don't *know* anything. I've told you there's a bizarre theory . . .'

'Whose? Who've you been talking to?' Stephen glared at him. 'I asked you here to help, not throw up more bloody mysteries!'

'All right,' Maltravers agreed. 'It's not fair and I'm sorry to have held out on you. I'll tell you as long as you agree not to say anything to Veronica – or anyone else – at this stage and you don't fly off the handle and start charging in like the Seventh Cavalry, however much you may want to. You're in danger of becoming too emotionally involved. Anyway, I'll now tell you about my chat with Sally Baker.'

'Sally Baker?'

'That's it. Shrewd lady.' Maltravers glanced towards the kitchen through which Dean had left. One thing he was not going to mention was his suspicion about Ursula and Bernard Quex; there was enough salacious gossip in Medmelton without him adding to it.

Chapter Ten

'Is Tess Davy about? OK, I'll hold. Thanks.'

Maltravers stood by the front-room window with his portable phone, looking at the tower of St Leonard's rising over Dymlight Cottage's high hedges. Stephen had remained very calm the previous evening, accepting Maltravers's insistence that the idea of Michelle being involved in the sinister churchyard rituals was still only a theory, and that there was nothing concrete at this stage. He had phoned the parents of the twins Michelle said she had gone to see with some spurious excuse that she might have left something behind. They confirmed she had been with their daughters, but had left some time before nine thirty – and they lived less than five minutes' walk away. So there was half an hour unaccounted for. She had not been dressed for hanging around the churchyard on an October night, so had she visited someone else? Stephen was going to check casually with another girl in the village, but Maltravers privately doubted that she had been with her. Michelle had told the truth; but saying where she had genuinely been for part of the evening was only cover for whatever else she had done – and that something else had sent her racing home in terror. Stephen was uneasy, but had agreed to leave the situation with Maltravers until something more definite emerged – if it ever did. Faced with walls of silence, Maltravers could think of nothing to do except agitate Medmelton's surface again.

'Hello, darling. How are you?' Sanity was a voice from BBC Bristol.

'Being chased by ghoulies and ghosties and long-legged beasties and things that go bump in the night.'

97

'What? You can't be pissed this early in the day.'

'Protective humour,' he explained. 'Have you got a few minutes?'

'I've got as long as you want. They're trying to untangle a snarl-up in editing. What's the matter?'

'I want to tell you some tales of ancient witchcraft in darkest Devon and how I have become persona decidedly non grata in Medmelton. If they still had stocks on the village green that's where I'd be calling from.'

'You're sounding paranoid, but I'm afraid it's another couple of days before I can come and stop them throwing things at you.'

'I'm not paranoid – they really are out to get me.'

'Oh, stop it!' Tess protested. 'I don't need this first thing in the morning. What are you raving about?'

Maltravers turned from the window and sprawled on the chaise-longue. 'Here beginneth the reading and you can ask questions at the end.'

It took twenty minutes to explain known facts, bizarre theories and his own thoughts, after which Tess was exploding with questions. Most of them he had already asked himself – and had no answers – but one leapt out at him like a light going on.

'Who *is* Michelle's father?'

'Why?' he demanded sharply, ahead of reasoning out implications.

'Because if you're right about suspecting that Patrick Gabriel wasn't bothered about the fact she was under the age of consent and her father learnt about it . . . come on, you can work it out yourself. But was he from Medmelton and does he still live there? Have you asked Stephen?'

'He doesn't know. Veronica's always refused to talk about it. To anybody. But . . . Michelle's birthday is some time in May, so if Veronica was here in . . . May, April, March . . . some time the previous August, then it could mean her father *is* from Medmelton.' Maltravers gave a grunt of frustration. 'But how do I find out?'

'If her parents are still around, ask her mother,' Tess advised.

'She'd be a very odd woman if she hadn't worked out the timing and tried to guess who it was. Have you met them?'

'No, but Stephen's told me where they live. He vaguely said we might call on them.'

'Take him up on it . . . and he might have discussed it with them anyway. It's all I can think of, but it's worth a try.'

'It certainly is,' Maltravers agreed. 'Good thinking, Batwoman. But it still leaves the question of what the hell's going on with Michelle and this damned Lazarus Tree.'

'That's really weird,' Tess said. 'Surely the kid can't believe in conjuring up the dead?'

'She believes in something – and somebody's leading her on. And it certainly can't be her father, whoever he is. That . . .'

'Hold on,' Tess interrupted. 'You say Veronica hasn't told *anybody* who he is. Not even Michelle?'

'Not as far as I know.'

'Well, when she's eighteen, she'll be legally entitled to find out for herself, of course.'

'She could find that difficult,' Maltravers said. 'Stephen once told me that her father's name doesn't appear on her birth certificate. Veronica simply refused to give it and there was no way to make her.'

'But Veronica must accept that Michelle's got a right to know,' Tess protested. 'What *is* she hiding, unless . . . just a cotton-pickin' minute! Why did Patrick Gabriel choose Medmelton to retreat to? How about he'd been there before . . . fifteen years ago, perhaps? Is what I'm thinking insane or am I just going too fast for you?'

'Don't be patronising . . . but it hadn't occurred to me,' Maltravers admitted. 'But there are a lot of holes in it. They remember strangers in Medmelton and I'm not aware of anyone suggesting that Gabriel had been here before. And even if he was Michelle's father, why didn't Veronica name him?'

'You know what she's like,' Tess commented. 'She keeps secrets for her own reasons. However, he comes back, meets Michelle . . . and perhaps incest is one of the things he hadn't tried. From what you've told me about Patrick Gabriel, it's horribly plausible.'

'Assuming, of course, that he knew about Michelle in the first place . . . but the more you think about it, the more preposterous it becomes. This was enough of a mess before I rang you.'

Tess hesitated. 'This woman you've been talking to told you that only a very few people have got a first edition of this Ralph the Talespinner character . . . what was her name again?'

'Sally Baker . . . and it makes perverse logic. But putting aside the copy in Exeter Library, only Bernard Quex, the rector, and some recluse couple are known to have it.'

'And you don't think the rector's squeaky clean . . . incidentally, how long has he been in Medmelton?'

'About twenty years . . .' Maltravers suddenly caught the tone of Tess's question. 'Are you now suggesting *he* could be Michelle's father? A moment ago it was Gabriel, for God's sake.'

'Well, it's obviously another option. You suspect he's having an affair with a married woman.' She chuckled. 'Perhaps he considers screwing parishioners among his benefits of clergy.'

'You've got a more jaundiced view of the church than I have.'

'When you've been propositioned – in the nicest possible way – by a curate at the age of sixteen, it tends to colour your judgement,' Tess replied sourly.

'I never knew that.'

'Well, I was . . . and your Mr Quex has got the book as well, hasn't he? Now there's a thought.'

Maltravers looked towards the window again. Everything centred around St Leonard's. The Lazarus Tree where Gabriel's body had been found, and where Quex had later discovered the strange offerings. The churchyard where Michelle spent time alone . . .

'But . . .' he began uncertainly, 'no, never mind the buts. You're right. The Reverend Quex is definitely in the frame – and he's a better bet than Gabriel. While I'm thinking about that, I want to start the village tom-toms beating again.'

'What are you planning this time?'

'Something that ought to produce results, although God knows what they'll be. Still got time to talk? Good. It's my turn to come up with mad ideas.'

*

Sally Baker arrived shortly after he finished the call. 'I'm assuming you're alone,' she said as she stepped through the front door.

'Everybody else is out,' he confirmed. 'I was about to come and see you in fact. But first of all, what's brought you here?'

'Do you realise they're talking about nothing but you in this village?'

Maltravers grinned. 'I rather gained that impression in the Raven last night. I've been stirring things up and am not Mr Popularity.'

'You don't know the half of it. Would you like the full list of the people you're about to arrest?'

'Arrest? Who the hell do they think I am?'

'You're . . . I'll try to remember them all . . . from Scotland Yard, Special Branch, MI5 or MI6 – nobody's quite sure which one deals with internal security – or Interpol. I don't think you made the SAS, but I may have missed that.'

'All that from dropping a hint to Mildred Thomson?' Maltravers looked intrigued. 'Feelings are tender round here. So whose collar am I about to start fingering?'

'Most of them you've never heard of, but I was in the Raven after you and Stephen left and the word was that you'd showed a particular interest in Gilbert Flyte. Can you remember meeting him?'

'Very clearly. He scuttled off almost as soon as we were introduced. His behaviour patterns were apparently all wrong, but I had no special interest. I'd never heard of him.'

'Well, he was only one of the names.' Sally Baker glanced at him. 'Have you come up with anything or are you just whistling in the dark?'

'And blind as a bat,' Maltravers admitted, then hesitated. 'Except for . . . I'll start with Bernard Quex. I think I've picked up something there and . . . I'm not totally convinced about this, but would you drop dead with shock if I suggested he was having an affair?'

'Really?' Interest flickered in Medmelton eyes. 'Who with?'

'Veronica's sister-in-law. I've not mentioned this to Stephen.'

'Ursula? Well, well, well.' Sally Baker nodded admiringly.

'You've certainly dug up something there. I've never heard any-body even obliquely suggest that. How sure are you?'

'Better than ninety-nine per cent. I don't think it can have been going on very long though – deception isn't their strong suit – but you don't seem particularly surprised.'

'Frankly, I'm not. Ewan Dean's as cold as charity and that marriage has looked distinctly dodgy for a long time. As for Bernard . . . well, the spirit is willing, et cetera.'

There was a matter-of-fact acceptance in the comment which Maltravers leapt on. 'Are you suggesting she's not the first?' Sally Baker looked surprised at the sharpness of the question.

'I don't want to give you the idea he's a rustic Casanova. I imagine his conscience punishes him for it. But . . .' She shrugged. 'Bernard's a widower in his early fifties and he's a rector, not a monk. Clerical collars don't have the same effect as bromide in the tea.'

'And do you think he might . . . how can I put this . . . operate within a small circle? A small family circle?' Maltravers asked blandly.

'You mean . . .' She shook her head uncertainly. 'Sorry, you'll have to spell it out.'

'I mean did he start with Veronica?'

'And he's Michelle's . . . ?' Now she followed him. 'No, I can't see that. Bernard's wife died only about ten years ago. I can't believe he fooled around before that . . . or is it now my turn to be naïve?'

'Not naïve,' Maltravers corrected. 'Just charitable. I haven't a shred of proof, but while Michelle certainly gets her Medmel-ton eyes from her mother, that midnight hair might come from both parents. Bernard's got black hair – and that could explain why Veronica's always refused to identify him. Incidentally, who else could it have been? Any ideas?'

'Only guesses. I wasn't living here when Michelle was born, but it was still a sort of low-key village scandal when I came back. I've heard various names, but it might be none of them.'

'What does Veronica's mother think?' Maltravers asked. 'I've just been talking to Tess about this – she's my partner who's due here in a couple of days – and she insists the grandmother must have tried to work it out. Do you know her?'

'I've known Kathleen for years – and she's often talked to me about it,' Sally confirmed. 'It still troubles her. She's classic Women's Institute country, never says anything stronger than "Damn – pardon my swearing". Veronica having an illegitimate child was bad enough without not producing the father so he could marry her.'

'And who did she think he was?'

'She's convinced herself it was a boy called Derek Williams who moved away from here years ago. But he was just one of a group of youngsters who were friends of Veronica and Ewan. They'd all grown up together, Sunday school, church youth club, a couple of them went to the same university. Kathleen had no proof that Derek was any more than just another member of the clan as far as Veronica was concerned – but she settled on him.'

'But why did it have to be somebody local?' Maltravers asked. 'Wasn't Veronica away at college? It could have been someone she met there.'

'Oh, Kathleen worked that out,' Sally told him. 'Michelle must have been conceived some time in August – and Veronica was home from university and living with her parents from the middle of July and all that month. It had to have happened while she was here.'

'But she can't have spent every moment in Medmelton,' Maltravers argued. 'She'd have gone to Exeter or Plymouth or . . . somewhere. Did she never spend a night away from home? She could have had some boyfriend she kept quiet about – that would be typical of her.'

'Kathleen insists she spent every night under their roof,' Sally told him. 'And, anyway, if she'd had a casual screw with a boyfriend – or even an affair with a married man – why not name him? Even if she didn't want to marry him, at least she could have made him pay maintenance.'

Maltravers's mouth twisted into a cynical moue. 'Because it would have been acutely embarrassing? Not any married man, but the respected and respectable rector of this parish.'

Sally suddenly looked troubled. 'All right, but what are you really hinting at, Gus? Because I don't think I like it.'

'The bottom line on this scenario is that Bernard is Michelle's father, Patrick Gabriel screwed her when she was under age, Bernard found out and killed him,' Maltravers replied levelly.

She was standing with her back to the window; now she turned and looked at the tower of St Leonard's. 'Bernard seducing a teenager – no, Veronica must have been nearly twenty-one at the time – and now a murderer? I need a few minutes to adjust to that.'

'You may not have to,' Maltravers said. 'I can't prove a word of it. And anyway, Tess came up with another suggestion which is even wilder, but that happens when there aren't any facts to go on. Try this.'

Sally's face went from intrigued to dismissive at the suggestion of an unknown affair between Veronica and Patrick Gabriel.

'No way,' she said firmly even before he had finished. 'For God's sake, you know what he was like. He was as unobtrusive as a fox in the chicken house. There's no way he could have been in Medmelton and nobody knew about it.'

'Not Medmelton then,' Maltravers suggested. 'Exeter perhaps or somewhere else near enough for Veronica to have met him. And if you're going to argue that there was no reason for her not to identify him, if they'd met casually in a pub or somewhere he could have called himself anything he wanted before a quick screw and leaving town.'

Sally shook her head. 'Veronica was never the type to jump into bed with total strangers. I can go along with Bernard – just about – but the Gabriel idea is out of sight.'

'So are a lot of things,' Maltravers commented. 'When Stephen asked me down here, I never imagined I'd end with a mess like this. I have the horrible feeling there will be tears before bed unless I decide it's none of my business and get the hell out.'

'But you won't. You told Stephen you'd help him, and if you quit now it won't just go away. He'd have to tackle it himself.' Sally smiled encouragingly. 'It's better that an outsider does it. It won't hurt you – at least not as much.'

'That's cold comfort,' he commented. 'But I expect you're right – and at the moment you're the one ally I've got on site. Stephen's too close to this to help.'

'Fair enough,' she agreed. 'What do you want me to do?'

'Lie.' Maltravers smiled sourly. 'Which shouldn't be too difficult for someone whose husband was in the diplomatic service.'

She pulled a face at him. 'Cynic – but accurate cynic. And there is someone else who might be able to help. Alexander Kerr. I met him through my husband – they belonged to the same club. He was a senior manager with the Post Office, but he's retired now and lives just down the hill from me. He's the sort who does abstruse crosswords and likes thinking up impossible puzzles – and he's another outsider of course.'

'How do you think he can help?'

'I think if you bounce any ideas you have off him, he might come up with something useful.'

Maltravers shrugged. 'If you think he's worth trying.'

'I'm sure he is. Look, he'll be at home now. Why don't we go there and talk it through?'

'Fine. I assume he's trustworthy.'

'Absolutely.'

And, Gus Maltravers, I've just shown how smoothly I can lie and you'll never know it, Sally Baker reflected to herself.

Standing by one of the clerks' desks, Gilbert Flyte flinched as he heard the voice speaking to a counter assistant. It had taken an enormous effort to concentrate his mind on work that morning, but for nearly half an hour the frantic worries had been held at bay. Now a recognised Medmelton voice brought them all rushing back and he jumped as though he had been bitten.

'Good morning, Gilbert.' Waiting while his shop takings were checked and deposited, Ewan Dean nodded through the glass partition. It was a regular transaction, but Flyte immediately leapt to mad conclusions. Ewan Dean was Stephen Hart's brother-in-law so this man . . . what was his name? . . . Mallory, Malcolm, Malsomething . . . was using him as a spy. My God, they were clever. What was he watching for? Be careful. He's probably been provided with one of their miniature tape recorders.

'Good morning.'

That was safe enough . . . but should he say something else? What would they read into silence? What did he usually say? Something about the weather? Ask how business was? Don't mention the family. That's what they wanted, something a skilled interrogator could pick up on. 'Why did you take such an interest in Mr Dean's family, Mr Flyte? Any particular member of the family was it? His wife . . . or his niece, perhaps? You do know his niece, don't you, Mr Flyte? Michelle. How well do you know her? Bit strange, isn't it, a man of your age knowing a teenage girl? I think there's something you haven't told us, isn't there . . . ?' As nightmares scampered through Flyte's imagination, Dean's impassive face began to blur behind the glass.

'Are you all right, Mr Flyte?'

'What!' Startled by the assistant's question, Flyte was aware that he had almost shouted.

'You don't look well. Do you want to sit down?'

'No. Of course not. I'm perfectly all right.' He agitatedly waved the statement he was holding. 'I'll handle this.'

The ten yards to the safety of his office was a passage through a fire of burning eyes and he was shaking as he leant back against the closed door. There was no escape. They were following him everywhere. How many of them were there? Hiding in vans taking photographs, sitting behind newspapers at the next table in the café where he invariably had lunch, relentless, professional, patient. If they'd hired Ewan Dean, how could he trust anyone he knew? What was happening in Medmelton while he was in Exeter? Had they got a warrant to search the cottage? Gilbert Flyte had to grab the handle of a filing cabinet, fingers painfully squeezing cold metal, to prevent himself from fainting. They were talking to Doreen . . . and to Mother. They would betray him. Not deliberately, but because they would be frightened and confused.

It mustn't happen here. Not at the bank. Not in front of the staff and Mr Hood. Not with customers watching. Would they let him put a blanket over his head as they led him to the car? It would make no difference. Everybody in Exeter would know. The Rotary Club, members of the Mayor's charity committee, the bank pension fund. Better to face it away from here. That was it. Confess enough to satisfy them, feed them something. Then ask for their discretion in return. No publicity – oh, *please* no publicity – a quiet early retirement on health grounds, then a move somewhere else. Surely it didn't have to be prison? A good barrister – he'd known Thomas Walters for years – would be able to argue mitigating circumstances. Dr Bennett would confirm the treatment he'd been receiving. There was his previous good character . . . but first he had to confess. Voluntarily. Quickly. Now. Where could he find – the name suddenly came back – Maltravers? Was he still in Medmelton? Even if he wasn't, Flyte wanted to get there before they arrived at his home. His mind began to clear as a decision was taken. Crossing to his desk, he flicked the intercom switch to his secretary.

'Miss Wellington?' Harpstring nerves tightened his voice. 'Miss Wellington, I'm afraid I'm not very well. I'm going home.'

'Oh, Mr Flyte. Is there anything I can do?'

'No. It's all right. I think it must have been something I ate. Will you let Mr Hood know? I'm leaving immediately.'

'Yes, of course, but . . .'

Flyte switched her off. He had to get out. Facing Mr Hood – or any of them – was impossible. It was highly irregular, but it didn't matter. He would never be coming back. He snatched his coat from the hanger and within a minute was out of the back entrance into the bank's private car park and had driven away. In his office, Miss Wellington looked in dismay at the papers uncleared from his desk. Poor Mr Flyte. It must be something very serious to make him leave like that.

At the bank counter, Ewan Dean smiled automatically as his deposit book was stamped and handed back to him; momentary interest in Flyte's abrupt retreat to his office had vanished. He'd known Gilbert and his neuroses for years and did all he could to avoid him. He walked back to his shop, removed the sign saying 'Back in ten minutes' from the door, then went to make a cup of coffee. Depressed by the recession, business was dire with only schoolchildren buying cheap aeroplane kits while serious modelmakers saved their money. The shop, which had been an escape, was becoming a burden of slow-moving stock, rising costs and crippling loan repayments. He never discussed it with Ursula of course – in fact he never discussed it with anyone. Self-reliant since earliest childhood, he wrapped it all close to himself, inner discipline treating rising problems with complete detachment. The casual affair with Miriam, his assistant until he could no longer afford her, had been as meaningless as going with a whore, basic satisfaction of a physical need. Dissatisfied and bored with her own marriage, she had been ideal for such an arrangement; once she had calmly served her own husband in the shop five minutes after a brief, eager grunting in the back room.

Standing by the chipped porcelain sink within a few feet of where they had coupled on a pile of flattened cardboard packing cases, Dean flicked drops off his coffee spoon as he tried to analyse what he was feeling. It was an emotion, but he found it difficult to recognise. He began to think that he was simply unhappy, such a vague, unquantifiable condition that the concept annoyed him. To admit you were unhappy meant that at some time you had been happy. What a stupid word. At various periods in his life, he had felt contented, satisfied, angry – certainly angry – smug, remorseful, even guilty. He had been in what was called love – but that was a long time ago – and he knew he had the capacity to hate. But what was happy? A sentiment for clowns and children, a spurious promise for dreamers – and Ewan Dean did not dream. He had a dead marriage, a business in difficulties and memories. He could handle that, he could live with it.

Chapter Eleven

'Mr Maltravers, you are a very devious man.' Alexander Kerr sounded approving rather than accusatory.

'That's not what most people who know me say,' Maltravers replied. 'I've been told that I can be inconveniently honest. It's considered a sort of inverted moral handicap. George Washington should have been a failure.'

'Then it's an excellent cover. Nobody suspects a man who's known to be truthful.' Kerr glanced towards Sally Baker, sitting on a padded carved settee in the window alcove of his front room. 'And will you be able to play your part in this deception?'

'I may not have to do very much,' she replied. 'But do you think it will get anywhere?'

'I can't see how it can avoid having some consequences – but don't ask me what they might be. You are, after all, guessing.'

Maltravers reached forward to offer a cigarette which Kerr accepted. 'And you haven't made any comment on my guesses,' he said. 'What do you think of them?'

'They're as plausible as anything, I expect, but that doesn't mean they're correct. You'll have to try it and see.'

'And what guesses would you make? You know Medmelton better than I do.'

Kerr intrigued Maltravers for reasons he could not pin down. Eyes alert as a stalking cat and with the same stillness as he listened, the neat, slight man could not avoid revealing a natural intelligence only amplified by what sounded like deliberately naïve comments. When he had arrived with Sally Baker, Maltravers had made polite conversation about retirement in Devon after a career in the Post Office and had caught a subtle evasiveness. Kerr had never married, so his job appeared to have been his life – but there had been no sense of loss at having left it, none of the usual disparaging remarks about how standards had fallen since his day, no recollections. It was very tenuous, faint notes so slightly off key that there was nothing Maltravers could pin down, but he felt that Alexander Kerr's abilities could have been put to better use than organising the delivery of the nation's mail, however elevated a position he had achieved in that service.

'Don't overestimate my knowledge of Medmelton. As Sally will tell you, I rarely leave my warren.' Kerr drew on his cigarette and tapped it unnecessarily over a glass ashtray. 'However, it strikes me that you might give a little more thought to other possible owners of this first edition of Ralph the Talespinner. You're concentrating on the ones you know – and once you've dismissed this reclusive couple, you're left with Bernard Quex. You add this supposed affair and an interesting theory about Michelle's paternity and . . .' He hesitated. 'Well, couldn't you be overlooking something else because what you've got can all be made to fit in some way?'

'I don't know anyone else who has the book,' Sally said.

'But who *might* have it?' Kerr queried. 'Quite a lot of people when you think about it. Some families have lived here for generations – a lot of families – and they hand things down.'

'On that basis, God knows how many people it could be,' she commented. 'Most of Medmelton.'

'True,' Kerr acknowledged. 'So whittle them down. Merely owning the book doesn't prove anything – you need one in the hands of a certain type of personality, one with a capacity for mischief. From your knowledge of the village, Sally, you can surely knock out quite a lot of options. Put it this way. Of those who could have the book, of how many would you think it *impossible* – or at least incredibly unlikely – for them to be playing at witchcraft or whatever this is?'

She was silent for a moment. 'About a dozen off the top of my head. I'll come up with more later.'

'Now look at it from the opposite direction,' Kerr said. 'Likely possibilities. Those with a long connection with Medmelton and who are perhaps – how shall we put it? – the sort of people where you wonder what they're really like. People who make you feel somehow uneasy, however well you know them.'

'I'd have to think about that.'

'Then do so.'

Maltravers was suddenly aware that it was as though he was no longer in the room. Kerr was speaking only to Sally, coaxing her mind, and she was starting to look slightly uncomfortable.

'I expect . . . well I could imagine anyone if I wanted to . . .' She shook her head. 'Alex, what are you trying to get me to say?'

'I want you to see. Try to look at it like an outsider.'

There was a silence before Maltravers spoke. 'I'm an outsider.'

'And do you have any suggestions?' Kerr was still looking at Sally.

'I don't know many people here, of course – but I find Mildred Thomson distinctly off-putting.'

Kerr turned towards him. 'I assume you've got more than her unfortunate appearance for saying that.'

'I think so. I think she's frustrated – not just sexually, but as a human being. She's lonely, she's not stupid and all that life offers her is gossip, people's sympathy and serving groceries until she dies.'

Kerr remained looking at him, but spoke to Sally. 'Any arguments with that analysis?'

'When did you work it out, Alex?' she asked.

'A long time ago, but it wasn't important. I shop there regularly and I've watched her gathering nuggets of people's lives. It even crossed my mind that she might blackmail someone. If we'd ever had an outbreak of poison pen letters in Medmelton, I could have told the police where they might start making inquiries.'

'And she is from a long-established family who could well have had a first edition of Ralph the Talespinner,' Maltravers added. 'You also are a devious man, Mr Kerr.'

Kerr laughed and the tension broke. 'I'm a bored old pensioner with nothing better to do than dream up fantasies about my neighbours. I don't know if I'm right about Mildred – I could be slandering her appallingly.'

'But you think we should bear her in mind,' Maltravers commented.

'For what it's worth – which may be absolutely nothing.' Kerr stood up. 'In the meantime, we'll have coffee. Back in a moment.' He left the room and they could hear him whistling in the kitchen.

'I like your friend,' Maltravers said. 'How did you meet him?'

'Through Peter – my husband. They were in the same club.'

'Oh yes, so you said.' Maltravers stubbed out his cigarette. 'And what about Mildred, then?'

'I don't know.' Sally appeared confused. 'She could . . . all right, it's possible she's putting this nonsense into Michelle's head, but I can't believe that she'd murder anyone.'

'Neither can I, because I can't see a reason. But if Michelle's playing at stupidities like conjuring up the dead, there's only one dead man who seems to fit. And someone murdered him.'

'So what are you going to do?'

'What we've already discussed because I can't think of anything else. And at least we'll be ready if Mildred floats to the surface.'

For a few minutes, the only sounds were of Kerr bustling in the kitchen. Sally stared out of the window and Maltravers idly glanced around the room. Instinctively, he read titles and authors in the open bookcase next to him; what appeared to be a complete set of Graham Greene; three volumes of Horace; Donne's Sermons; *Don Quixote* in Spanish; Copernicus's *De Revolutionibus Orbium*; Molière and De Quincey. Alexander Kerr had been a very literate postman. On the bottom shelf was what looked like a first edition of *Call for the Dead* – the only Le Carré Maltravers lacked from his own collection – and he reached across to pull it out and check. It was a first edition and had a handwritten inscription on the title page: 'To Alex Kerr – recognise anyone? D. C. June 5, 1961.' Maltravers smiled to himself and put the book back just before Kerr returned.

'A penny's just dropped,' he said as he placed a plastic tray with coffee and biscuits on an occasional table. 'Somebody once told me that Mildred Thomson's mother used to read the Tarot. Might be nothing in it, but it could be another bit of the puzzle.'

'The trouble is that we can't see why she should want to murder Patrick Gabriel,' Maltravers said.

'Nobody can see why anyone wanted to.' Kerr handed Sally her cup. 'There were endless theories – although your suggestion that it could have been Michelle's father, whoever he is, never came up to my knowledge. All options are open, including some nobody's thought of.'

'Then let's hear some of yours,' Maltravers suggested.

'Mine?' Kerr laughed dismissively. 'This isn't my business and if you choose to make it yours, that's nothing to do with me either. Frankly, I'd much rather talk about your writing, Mr Maltravers. I enjoyed *Burnt Offerings* tremendously. All imagination, or did autobiography creep in?'

Kerr was not to be moved back to Medmelton affairs and Maltravers indulged in the pleasurable conceit of talking about his own work while they drank their coffee. But he noted the understated probing that went deeper than a detached discussion of his books and plays, encouraging him to reveal more about himself than he consciously allowed out in his writing.

'What exactly was your job with the Post Office?' he suddenly asked.

'When I retired, I had the wondrous title of Divisional Postmaster South-west Region, brackets Outer London close brackets. It sounds incredibly important, but was actually no more than pushing pieces of paper around until they disappeared into some happy limbo.'

'It sounds like a waste of a good Cambridge degree,' Maltravers commented.

The flame of Kerr's gold-plated lighter paused as he raised it to another cigarette and his eyes narrowed. 'Did Sally mention that to you?'

'No.' Maltravers indicated a framed photograph on a rolltop desk across the room. 'But you were cox for the Boat Race crew in nineteen . . . I can't quite see the full date. What did you read?'

'Classics – and I got a First.' Kerr finished lighting the

cigarette. 'However, that was a long time ago. Were you there?'

'No, nor any other university. I had endless arguments with my father who wanted me to go, but I was determined to become a journalist.' Maltravers stood up. 'Anyway, I must be off. It's been a pleasure meeting you.'

'And meeting you. I'll see you out. Can you hang on a minute, Sally?'

Without waiting for a reply, Kerr led Maltravers to the front door and returned looking thoughtful.

'"Blades of Sheffield is sharp",' he remarked drily.

'You don't think he suspects anything, do you?' Sally sounded concerned. 'About you?'

'Mr Maltravers certainly doesn't believe I was a postman . . .' Kerr sat down and tapped the fingers of one hand against the fist of the other. 'But I think we can rely on his discretion, so there's nothing to worry about . . . and he may have enough wit to solve Medmelton's little local mystery. I hope for his sake that he doesn't find it painful.'

'Would that bother him?' Sally asked.

'Oh, yes. With the right training, he could have worked with my people – but that sentimental streak would have made him a dangerous liability.'

Gilbert Flyte's panic was becoming terminal. Simply being in his car driving home before lunchtime was so alien to the orderly processes of his life that it added its own disorientation. Another car followed him for half a mile, imagined menace in the rear view mirror growing with every second, until he swerved abruptly into a layby and let it pass, gibbering the registration number to himself as he scrabbled in the glove compartment for a piece of paper on which to write it down. But it made no difference. They'd have dozens of vehicles tightening the net; what use was the number of one of them? And stopping was disastrous, giving them more vital minutes to search and question. As he pulled out, the blast of a horn howled behind him and a juggernaut's air brakes oozed violently. Blind to the looming shape inches from his bumper, Flyte sped on, sobbing. By the time he reached the Medmelton turn, he was trembling and twice scraped the car's endlessly polished bodywork against the roadside hedges. As he raced down the hill, the sight of Maltravers walking back towards the village produced an irrational sense of relief. He braked violently and leapt out of the car, leaning against it panting as his tormentor approached.

'All right!' he gasped. 'I'll tell you.'

Still several yards away, Maltravers made a rapid adjustment to the totally unexpected, using the distance between them for thinking time. He wondered which one of several possible branches of authority Flyte believed he belonged to.

'Tell me what, Mr Flyte?' he asked cautiously.

'Everything. Where do you want to take me?'

'We can talk here for a moment.'

Flyte's breath stuttered and he croaked with fear. This was how they did it, of course. Casually at first, fishing for indiscretion. Well, he wasn't going to be played with. He just wanted it out in the open.

'Aren't you going to record it? Write it down?'

'No need for that yet.' Maltravers smiled slightly. 'You look as though you need to sit down. Shall we get into the car?'

Flyte obeyed automatically, sitting in the driver's seat, staring straight ahead. He jumped as Maltravers tapped on the passenger door window.

'Could you unlock the door, please? Thank you.' Maltravers sat beside him. 'Take your time, Mr Flyte. There's no hurry.'

As the terrified man remained silent, Maltravers tried to work out what was happening. He knew virtually nothing about Flyte and their one meeting had been very brief. He had turned the virtue of orderliness into the vice of an obsession but was otherwise an apparently harmless inadequate. What had brought all this on? And what was 'it'?

'Can it be kept quiet?' Still staring straight ahead, Flyte had started to cry.

'That's not for me to decide.' Maltravers suddenly felt sorry for him. Whatever he was about to confess was crucifying him with guilt. 'Just tell me everything. From the beginning.'

Flyte sniffed. 'I knew it was wrong, but I didn't think I was doing any harm. I don't know why I did it. It's very . . . I felt bad afterwards. Ashamed. I have a position. At the bank.' He turned to him urgently. 'Please . . . it's my mother, you see. And Doreen.'

Maltravers suppressed an urge of sympathy with an edge to his voice. 'Mr Flyte, I can't promise anything until you tell me exactly what you have done.'

Flyte fumbled in his pocket and produced that day's spotless linen handkerchief with his initials embroidered in one corner, wiping away tears then blowing his nose noisily. The action seemed partially to control him.

'I bought the telescope in Plymouth,' he began unexpectedly. 'A lot of shops there sell them. It was for bird-watching, but then I began to . . . to use it round the village. It's very powerful and you can see all sorts of things. I mean . . . into people's houses. And . . . and there are special lenses that work at night.'

Maltravers wound down the window and lit a cigarette, light partially dawning, but wondering where this was all leading. 'Go on.'

'There wasn't much at first. People leaving the Raven, coming home late at night. And sometimes in the summer, people didn't draw their curtains . . . their bedroom curtains.' Flyte swallowed nervously and looked down. 'This is very embarrassing for me.'

'It's best that you tell me,' Maltravers prompted. 'Everything.'

'One night . . . I can't remember the date, which isn't like me . . . I saw a movement in the churchyard. I looked across the green and saw . . . the moon was quite bright . . . and I saw it was Michelle Dean. It was very late and I wondered what she was doing. She was alone, just sitting on the ground leaning against one of the tombs. Then Patrick Gabriel – the poet, you know all about him – came from behind the church and they started to . . .' Flyte lowered his head and there was a very long silence. Maltravers had to force him through the next stage.

'They started to have *sex*, Mr Flyte? Is that what they did? And you watched them?' The mumbled admission was barely audible. 'And this must have been about eighteen months ago when Patrick Gabriel was staying in Medmelton. Do you know how old Michelle Dean would have been then? Fourteen, Mr Flyte. Which means that you witnessed a criminal act –

however willing she was. Did you tell the police about it?'

'I couldn't!' Flyte protested desperately. 'I'd have had to explain how I knew about it and . . . and everything else would have come out.'

'So what did you do? Waited until you could watch them again?'

Flyte's face filled with shame. 'Yes. It happened several times, and I couldn't resist the . . .'

Maltravers let him cry. Confused and frightened, Flyte had presented him with the proof of what he had suspected about Gabriel's behaviour – although he doubted that Michelle Dean had begun her personal sex life with him. The least he could do was offer the pitiful little man a possible escape by playing on his spurious temporary reputation as an authority figure.

'You've done the right thing in telling me, Mr Flyte,' he said. 'I can't promise, but this may not have to go any further – as long as I have your assurance that you will never do this sort of thing again. Will you give me that assurance?'

Flyte shook his head helplessly. 'You don't understand. I've stopped doing it. I haven't done it since the night I saw him killed!'

Having thought he understood what was happening, Maltravers had difficulty controlling his reaction. Was Flyte lying to give his pompous personality a twist of self-importance? Was he really so psychologically weakened that public humiliation would become a sort of perverse fame? It was impossible to tell. But if that had been his case of need, he could have admitted this long ago, whereas the naked terror in his face revealed that confession was tearing him apart.

'The night you saw him killed,' Maltravers repeated. 'That's . . . rather more important. Tell me what happened.'

Flyte licked his lips. 'They hadn't been there for a couple of nights and I nearly didn't watch. But about a quarter past midnight – did I say it was always around that time? . . . anyway, I saw Gabriel arrive. He sat on one of the barrel tombs near the Lazarus Tree and began to smoke a cigarette. I saw his face when he lit it – it was overcast that night and the light was very poor. After a few minutes, I saw . . . obviously I thought it

117

was Michelle, but it wasn't . . . approaching from behind him. Gabriel must have heard them, because he stood up. I realised it couldn't have been her when they didn't immediately kiss each other.'

He glanced at Maltravers apologetically before continuing. 'They seemed to talk for a few moments, then this . . . this figure . . . it was hard to say exactly what happened, but they seemed to lunge at Gabriel and he fell down.'

'Just a minute,' Maltravers interrupted. 'You keep saying "figure" and "they". A man or a woman?'

'I couldn't tell. They were wearing trousers, but that didn't prove anything. I think they were about the same height as Gabriel.' Flyte answered hurriedly, as if anxious to finish what he had to say. 'Anyway, he or she bent down . . . as though they were . . . well, afterwards I realised they must have been making sure he was dead. Then they walked away.'

'In which direction?'

'I'm not sure . . .' Flyte swallowed and it seemed to hurt him. 'I knew something terrible had happened and I was shaking. I *think* it could have been towards the side of the church, but I might be wrong . . . I didn't sleep that night.'

Maltravers took a long draw on his cigarette as Flyte stopped abruptly. 'Were you questioned by the police after the murder?'

'Of course I was . . . and I didn't refuse to give my fingerprints.' Flyte offered the information as hesitant evidence that at least part of his behaviour had been correct. 'It was bad enough not telling them what I'd seen, without making them more suspicious.'

'Did you tell anyone? Your wife?'

'Doreen! God, no! Please, Mr . . . Mr . . . Maltravers, isn't it? I'm sorry, I don't know your official rank. I've told you now. I've told you everything I know. If I could say who did it, I would. Believe me. But if Doreen or my mother learns about this . . .' He began to weep again.

Maltravers turned to flick his cigarette end on to the roadside. Pressing Flyte to remember anything else at that moment would be both unkind and useless; everything had come bursting out like a festering abscess inside him and he was exhausted. And there was no point in continuing the charade.

'Mr Flyte, I have to admit something as well,' he said. 'I don't know what you think I am, but the fact is that I'm an ordinary private citizen like you. I am not from the police or anyone else.'

'What?' It was impossible to say if Flyte's reaction was simple amazement or dismay at what misunderstanding and terror had driven him to do. 'But in the Raven the other night, they said you were from London!'

Maltravers shrugged. 'So are a lot of people.'

'Not just from London! From Scotland Yard or . . . well, somewhere important. Official.'

'Well, I'm not,' Maltravers said. 'And it's not my fault if people's imaginations start running riot.'

'You should have told me. Right at the start.' Scrambling for some retreat, the haughty deputy bank manager began to surface. 'You've deceived me. It's intolerable. I've a good mind to . . .'

'A good mind to what?' Maltravers snapped impatiently. 'You deceived yourself – like a few other people seem to have done.'

'Then I'm going to tell them!' Flyte was switching into look-here-this-sort-of-thing-won't-do-at-all-you-know mode until Maltravers punctured his bombast.

'Oh, for Christ's sake! If you say anything to anybody, I'll go straight to the police and tell them everything you've just admitted to me. And they're not going to be bothered about your precious reputation, your wife or your mother!'

'I'll deny it.'

'How did anybody so stupid ever make it to assistant bank manager?' Maltravers said reflectively. 'Just use what we'll charitably refer to as your brain for a moment.' He stared impassively as Flyte began almost visibly to deflate, then he looked away.

'So what are you going to do? You have been taking an interest in the murder, haven't you?'

'Yes – and I'll keep the reasons to myself. What I'm going to do isn't your business, but we'll lay down a few ground rules. First of all, have you told me everything?'

'I wish I hadn't, but yes,' Flyte admitted bitterly.

'Then for the time being, I'll keep quiet about it . . . oh, yes, I mean it, although I'm not promising the situation won't change. You've withheld evidence from the police and been a dirty old man. Your best hope is that this can be sorted out without your becoming involved.'

'I can't see how that can be done.'

'Neither can I,' Maltravers admitted. 'But it's the only chance you've got. You've no choice but to trust me.'

'But what are you . . . ?'

'No questions,' Maltravers interrupted. 'Just accept that I'm dealing with it in my own way. And I might be able to do that without revealing your sordid nocturnal hobbies. In the meantime, keep your mouth shut – and sell that bloody telescope.'

He pulled the car door handle and began to step out, then stopped as something occurred to him. 'How long have you lived in Medmelton?'

Flyte appeared both surprised and suspicious. 'Pardon? It'll be twenty-three years next month. Why?'

Maltravers settled on the seat again, his feet on the grass verge. 'Do you have a copy of Ralph the Talespinner's stories?'

'Ralph the Talespinner?' Flyte certainly seemed bewildered. 'Yes, I have, but I don't see . . . ?'

'The first edition?'

'Yes. I bought it at a church jumble sale. What's all this about?'

'And you've read it?' Maltravers pressed.

'Not for years.' He managed to summon up an air of offence. 'I don't have to answer your questions, you know. You've no right to . . .'

'I could be at Exeter Police Station in less than half an hour,' Maltravers warned tersely. 'You can answer their questions instead if you like. It makes no difference to me.' Flyte blinked, rapidly and nervously. 'I've got my reasons for asking this, and that's all you need to know. Is there . . . any story you particularly remember?' It was better not to come straight out with it. If Flyte was the one playing grotesque games with Michelle, he would probably blab it out the moment he realised that Maltravers was suspicious.

'Which particular story?' he asked cautiously.

'You tell me.'

'No . . . no, I don't think I can remember any of them. I can't see the point of all this.'

'Well, there is one.' Maltravers stepped out of the car, then leant down to look back. 'Anyway, keep quiet about all this. One word out of line, and the proverbial hits the fan. Goodbye, Mr Flyte.'

Flyte started the engine almost simultaneously with the slamming of the door, and Maltravers watched him drive away. Genuine confession or desperate lie to conceal something worse? Better to be disgraced for distasteful habits and withholding evidence from the police than jailed for murder? But what reason could Flyte have had? Had Gabriel publicly insulted him in his cups one night in the Raven, fatally offending that pompous conceit? It seemed incredibly unlikely – but Flyte had shown he was capable of irrational behaviour, so to what degree might it extend? On reflection, the incident conjured up as many unanswered questions as questionable answers.

Chapter Twelve

Settled on the wooden sill of the staffroom window, the fly raised its front legs and rubbed them together like human hands anticipating excitement. It balanced forwards and stroked its back legs over the sheen of each wing in turn before buzzing frantically against the glass for a moment then landing again and repeating the whole process. Sipping his coffee from a chipped Exeter Cathedral souvenir mug, Stephen Hart watched it blankly. Flies scavenged in filth, but kept themselves clean. Corruption attracted them, but only for survival. If you put one in a sealed chamber with fresh food at one end and something rotting at the other, which would it choose? Did that mean . . . ? Suddenly irritated by meaningless thoughts, he flicked his hand and the creature flew off.

Beyond the window, school yard and playing fields were filled with children on mid-morning break. Younger ones were hyperactive, playing football, fighting, chasing each other, simply running about to burn off boisterous energy; older ones walked, lounged, leant against walls, lethargic, almost sullen in some cases, talking. Michelle was with a group of her classmates on the edge of the field. She was lying on her back, head on her schoolbag with its worn image of Billy Joel, right ankle balanced on the opposite raised knee, indifferent to or unaware of how her grey pleated skirt fell away from her legs, arm shielding her eyes from the sun. Abruptly, she sat up, turning to one of the boys and starting to talk animatedly. Perhaps he had said something that had annoyed or interested her. In the few minutes Hart watched, she said more than she would in an entire evening at home. Why wouldn't she talk to him? He'd always been conscious of her resentment at his arrival in her – and Veronica's – life, and had done all he could to open up communication and forge some kind of relationship. Did he love her? He wanted to, but it had not been possible. But he wanted to like her. He had first introduced himself to her as Stephen and she had never shown any wish to call him Dad. Did that matter? Rationally, no; emotionally, for all his rejection of the feeling, yes.

He suddenly realised that the boy she was talking to – Michael Scala, whose parents were Italian – looked like that waiter at the hotel in Greece. Michelle had been angry when by chance he and Veronica had found them together in her room, both almost naked but apparently not having completed what had begun. She had been indifferent to warnings about the risk of pregnancy or worse and had sulked over the strict limitations they placed on her for the remainder of the holiday. One evening – for some reason Veronica had not been with them – she had suddenly flared at him: 'He wouldn't have been the first, you know. I'm not your little virgin stepdaughter.' She had waited defiantly for a reaction and had looked shocked when he said, 'I know that. But you're still under age. So I'm going to have to play the wicked stepfather, aren't I?'

Afterwards, his reaction to what he had said had been confused; he had sounded like his own father. Respectability – that despised, middle-class, middle-aged totem of convention – had invaded him so insidiously that he had not been aware of it. Mortgage, life assurance, pension plan, career structure, building society account, even shares in British Gas, hung about him like badges of compromise. He had joined the class whose overthrow he had once demanded.

'Steve! There you are.' Anne Collins, the deputy head, sounded relieved. 'Jim Creasey's ill. Can you take 2H in your free period after lunch? Just give them something to read.' Without waiting for a reply, she added a tick to her clipboard then tapped it with her pen. 'That just leaves . . . Maggie! Could you possibly . . . ?'

Bustling and organising, she was gone. The bell rang for the end of break and Steve finished his coffee. Fiery ambitions to revolutionise education had been replaced by timetable problems and the tedium of teaching punctuation to bored third-formers.

'What have you been doing with yourself?' Veronica asked as she hung her anorak on one of the hooks by the front door.

Maltravers abandoned an infuriatingly tricky *Guardian* crossword. 'Being idle. Looked round the church, had lunch in the pub, then wandered out the other side of the village to commune with nature.'

'Did you get the chops all right?'

'I did not.'

'Oh, Gus! You promised you'd remember. Anyway, there's still time for me to . . .'

'I didn't say I forgot,' he corrected. 'I decided you ought to have a night off from cooking. I'm taking you and Stephen out to dinner. I've booked a table at the Royal Clarence in Exeter.'

'The Royal Clarence?' Veronica sounded impressed. 'That's in the cathedral close. Super place. How did you know about it?'

'I ran into Sally Baker and asked her to recommend somewhere. I also checked your kitchen calendar and neither of you appears to have anything on tonight. If it's really impossible, I can always cancel and get a takeaway instead.'

'No, it's fine . . . but why not wait until Tess arrives? When's she coming, incidentally?'

'Tomorrow afternoon,' he replied. 'I rang her this morning. But she's got friends near Plymouth she wants to visit tomorrow night and you or Stephen both seem to be tied up on the other evenings we'll be here. If I don't take you out tonight, I can't do it at all. I thought of booking for four, but it would probably bore Michelle spitless. Will she be all right on her own? We should be back about ten.'

'She'll be fine.' Veronica examined herself critically in a long Victorian mirror. 'I must shower and wash my hair. What time did you book for?'

'Table at seven thirty and I told them we'd arrive about seven for drinks . . . how long does your hair take to dry?'

'Not that long, but I'd better get on with it. I'll just organise supper for Michelle and make sure Stephen's got a clean shirt.'

Stephen and Michelle came home twenty minutes later. Pausing only to help herself to a bag of crisps and a glass of Coke from the kitchen, Michelle disappeared to her room with slightly tetchy promises to do her homework. When Maltravers asked if she minded them going out, she seemed surprised that he should think it would bother her.

'Anything happened?' Stephen asked when they were alone.

'Nothing dramatic,' Maltravers told him. 'After all, my activities are somewhat restricted. I met Sally Baker again and she introduced me to another of your neighbours, Alexander Kerr.'

'Alex? What did you think of him?'

'He's very . . . subtle. And I'm not altogether sure that I'd trust him — in the nicest possible way.' Maltravers decided not to tell Stephen about the inscription in the Le Carré book. He could be completely wrong about what it had suggested to him — and if he was right, Kerr would have very good reasons for passing himself off as an anonymous retired Post Office official. 'Anyway, he came up with an interesting idea about who might be behind this churchyard farce. Mildred Thomson.'

'Mildred? What makes him say that?'

'His reasoning doesn't matter — and it's only a suggestion in any event. What do you think?'

Stephen thought for a moment. 'I'm not sure. Mildred's been here for ever, she's just part of the scenery. She's always seemed harmless enough.'

Maltravers made an ambivalent sniff. 'Perhaps she is. But I'm bearing her in mind.'

'But what's the connection with Patrick Gabriel?' Stephen demanded.

'You told me that Gabriel bought his groceries from the stores while he was staying here,' Maltravers pointed out. 'So that's how they met — and if Alex Kerr's right, there could be a rather sinister side to your local village shopkeeper, in fact she might turn out to be very nasty. Which means that Gabriel could have recognised a kindred spirit and what happened after that is anybody's guess.'

'And how did Michelle become mixed up in it?' Stephen's voice had gone very quiet.

'I don't know.' Maltravers stopped as Veronica came back into the room, long wet hair clinging to her white towelling robe. 'Will that really be dry in time?'

'Of course it will.' She held up the shirt she was carrying. 'This needs ironing. Has Gus told you he's taking us out to dinner?'

'Yes. Michelle doesn't want to come.'

'I never imagined she would.'

As Veronica walked into the kitchen, Maltravers tapped the pockets of his jacket. 'I'm out of cigarettes again. Fancy a stroll to the stores?' As he spoke, he nodded silently at Stephen.

'Oh . . . yes, fine.' He raised his voice. 'Do we need anything from Mildred's?'

'Not now we're going out,' Veronica replied. 'See you soon.'

The two men did not speak again until they had reached the end of the lane and were crossing the ford.

'And what mustn't Veronica hear now?' Stephen asked.

'Tricky country, this one,' Maltravers told him. 'I spoke to Tess earlier and she came up with something that's . . . well, let's just say it's plausible. The problem is that I don't think you can come up with the answer to the key question here . . . you still have no idea who Michelle's father could be, have you?'

'I've told you that. Veronica's never revealed it. What's the point of bringing it up again?'

Maltravers sighed as if reluctant to continue. 'Look, this is no more than a theory and it could be completely out of line, but it's . . . well I can't just throw it out because I don't like it. It presupposes all sorts of things that might not be . . .'

Stephen stopped. 'Spit it out, Gus. I don't care what it is, I want to hear it. Right?'

'Sorry,' Maltravers apologised. 'Just accept the caveat that I'm not saying any of this is true.'

'Accepted. Now get on with it.'

He made no protests or interruptions, and when Maltravers

126

finished he removed his glasses, closed his eyes and pressed his fingers against the bridge of his nose. For several moments he did not speak.

'I've thought of worse possibilities,' he said finally.

'Like what?'

'They don't matter.' He blinked as he replaced his glasses. 'I'm not going to give you any arguments. I can quite believe Michelle had it away with Patrick Gabriel – and bloody Gilbert Flyte seeing them has almost a touch of farce about it.' He shook his head. 'As for your suggestion that Bernard could be her father . . . Jesus. But I can't tell you it's wrong. I don't know who her father is, where he is, even *if* he is. He could be dead for all I know.'

'Well, that's what's come bubbling out,' Maltravers told him. 'But even assuming there's a shred of truth in it, I can't see any way of proving it.'

'Then forget it. Nobody on God's earth will get that name out of Veronica. Simple as that. Unless you come up with another idea, there's nothing else we can do. Apart from this churchyard crap . . . and I'll sort out Mildred Thomson.'

'No,' Maltravers said sharply. 'Not yet. Alex Kerr suggested it could be her, but there's nothing at all to prove it.'

'So what the hell do you expect me to do?' Stephen snapped. 'Let her carry on corrupting the kid?'

'No, but let me handle it.'

'How?'

'Don't ask.' Maltravers held up his hand to stop further questions. 'You're too involved. I don't want to say any more at the moment. Just leave it with me for the time being and trust me. All right?'

When agreement finally came, it was very reluctant. 'All right . . . but how long will it take?'

'I'm not sure, but it could be fairly soon.'

'It better had be.'

It was a quarter past ten when they returned to Dymlight Cottage, Stephen and Veronica laughing as they stepped out of the car at the conclusion of a story Maltravers had been telling about one of the theatre's more eccentric characters.

'I fancy a nightcap,' he announced. 'Let's stroll over to the Raven.'

'Not for me,' Veronica said. 'I'd better make sure Michelle's all right. You two go ahead though. Lovely dinner, Gus. Thank you.'

'My pleasure. See you shortly.'

The evening was dank as they walked across the green, pink pub lights on steamed windows glowing like embers in the darkness. Maltravers began another story, finishing it just as they reached the bar. Sally Baker was among about a dozen customers and Stephen sat on the stool next to her as Maltravers ordered their drinks.

'Hello,' she said. 'Did your visitor find you all right?'

'What visitor? We've only just got back. Who was it?'

'Oh, yes, Gus told me he was taking you out,' she recalled. 'I don't know who she was. She just came in here and asked for directions to Dymlight Cottage.'

'She?' he repeated. 'When was this?'

'I'm not sure. I hadn't been here long, so it must have been around half past eight.' She turned to the woman behind the bar pouring Maltravers's wine. 'Julie, what time did that woman come in? The one who wanted to know where Dymlight Cottage was. You spoke to her.'

The landlady appeared to welcome being asked. 'Middle of the evening some time.'

'Did you recognise her?' Stephen queried.

'Never seen her.' She placed Maltravers's wine on the bar and began to pull Stephen's bitter. 'But she was from these parts sure enough.'

'How do you know?'

'Medmelton eyes. You couldn't miss them.'

'What did she say exactly?' Stephen pressed. 'Did she ask for us by name?'

'No . . . no, I don't think so. Just asked where your cottage was.' The pint was pulled. 'It struck me later that she ought to know if she came from Medmelton. Two pounds sixteen, please.'

'And one for yourself.' Maltravers handed her a five-pound note. 'Can you remember anything else about her? How old was she?'

'Difficult to say. Thirties, perhaps? Attractive as far as I could see, but she was wearing a headscarf and her coat was buttoned up.' She gave Maltravers his change. 'There you are. It's just a shandy for me. Thanks . . . oh, yes, there was one thing. She had a birthmark on her face − well, not her face precisely, I could only see the edge of it because it was hidden by the scarf. More on her neck it must have been − you know, that raspberry colour.'

'And she definitely had Medmelton eyes,' Maltravers repeated.

'I noticed that,' Sally put in. 'And they were very striking.'

The landlady was about to move to another customer when Maltravers stopped her. 'Can you remember any girl born here who had a birthmark like that? Someone who moved away?'

She shook her head firmly. 'No. There was a boy once − what was his name? Tommy something − who had a little one on his chin. But I don't know of anyone with one like she had. Excuse me.'

Maltravers picked up his drink and stood slightly away from the bar between Sally Baker and Stephen. 'How odd. Pity we were out tonight.'

'But who was she?' Stephen demanded.

'Obviously someone with local connections,' Maltravers said. 'Although she might not have been born here and the eyes could be some ancestral throwback.'

'But why did she suddenly turn up looking for Dymlight Cottage?' Sally demanded.

Maltravers shrugged. 'Perhaps it was her family's home years back and she wanted to visit it.'

'Out of the blue on an October night?' She sounded highly sceptical.

'Point taken,' Maltravers acknowledged. He looked casually

round the room and several heads turned away from him. 'What did the rest of the locals make of her?'

'She certainly interested them.' Sally dropped her voice. 'The place was fairly full and there was quite a bit of chat after she left. A few family resemblances were put forward, but it was all guesswork. You could hardly see her face and she was only in here a couple of minutes.'

'Well, Michelle would have met her if she went to the cottage,' Maltravers commented. 'She should be able to explain. In the meantime, there are enough mysteries round here without looking for any new ones. I'm sticking with my old family homestead theory.'

He thanked Sally for recommending the Royal Clarence and began talking about their meal, but Stephen remained silent. When Maltravers suggested another drink, he refused and said he wanted to get back.

'All right, if it's worrying you,' Maltravers agreed. 'Let's see if we can find out what it's all about. Goodnight, Sally.'

Conversation dropped perceptibly for a moment as they left with the weight of wary eyes on them; Medmelton was relishing a glut of material for gossip and rumour, but Maltravers wondered how much fear was mixed up in it. As they walked back through the night, concern seeped out of Stephen's silence.

'What are you thinking?' Maltravers asked quietly.

'I don't know. I just don't like it.' He did not look at him.

Carrying two glasses of water on a tray, Veronica was in her dressing gown at the foot of the stairs as they walked in.

'Is Michelle asleep?' Stephen asked sharply.

'Not yet. I'm just going to tell her to turn her light off.'

'Did she say anyone had been here this evening?'

'No. Why?'

'Gus'll tell you.'

Veronica looked startled as he pushed past her and hurried upstairs. 'What's happened?'

'There's been a stranger in the camp,' Maltravers explained as he watched Stephen disappear. 'I don't think it's anything, but Stephen's worried. Sit down for a minute.'

She put the tray on the bottom step as he moved towards the

fireplace. When he looked at her again, she was in the shallow rocking chair she always used, frowning questions at him.

'We met Sally Baker in the pub . . .'

The frowns deepened slightly as he told her, but when he finished she appeared indifferent. 'So what's he getting in a state about? Nothing's happened. Michelle's all right.'

'He didn't know that until we got back,' Maltravers pointed out.

'Well, she's fine,' Veronica said dismissively. 'If there'd been anything wrong, I'd have telephoned him at . . .' She broke off as Stephen came downstairs again. 'Gus has told me. There's no problem.' Maltravers noted the glance they exchanged; there was a great deal of distance in it. 'Did anyone call?'

Stephen shook his head. 'She says not, but she was out for about an hour.'

'Then stop panicking.' Veronica stood up and smiled at Maltravers. 'Thanks again for a lovely evening, Gus. See you in the morning.'

'For God's sake, doesn't anything get to you?' Stephen's voice snapped across some knife-edge of tension.

'Yes it does. But I don't go into a tailspin over it. I don't come barging in and upsetting my daughter with stupid questions. And I don't like you doing it!'

'Hold it right there,' Maltravers interrupted sharply. 'Before you both start throwing things.'

'I'm not about to throw things,' Veronica said calmly. 'I'm going to bed. Goodnight.' She walked past her husband without looking at him. Maltravers lit a cigarette to leave a space in which the temperature could drop.

'She's right,' he remarked. 'Michelle's perfectly safe – and if she was out for part of the evening, the woman could just have gone away when she found the house was empty.'

'But what did she want?' Stephen demanded.

'Who knows? If it was important, she'll turn up again. I'm beginning to regret taking you out tonight. If we'd been at home, it would all have been sorted out . . . Stephen, who do you think it was?'

He gestured helplessly. 'I don't know . . . it's just . . . you know what I'm concerned about, Gus! Michelle's up to something and I don't know what it is. Total strangers appearing could mean anything.'

'All right, all right,' Maltravers said soothingly. 'The trouble is that you and Veronica are poles apart over anything like this. It's fire and ice country. But look at it logically. If this woman had been up to anything sinister, she'd hardly have walked into a crowded pub where people would remember her, would she? And having found nobody in when she came here, she'll come back. If she does, you'll find out what it's about. If she doesn't . . . all right, you've got a mystery, but I can't see any immediate danger in it.

'Look. I'll call Sally Baker tomorrow and ask her to make a few casual inquiries — it's not the sort of thing I can do. She can ask in the stores and around the village if anyone else met this woman. If they did, she might have said more to them. I'll let you know anything she finds out. OK? In the meantime, stop the nightmare scenarios.'

Stephen sighed. 'What the fuck is going on, Gus?'

'I don't know — and neither do you. But, whatever it is, it won't be sorted out by you getting neurotic. Go to bed. I'll wait down here until you've finished in the bathroom.'

Stephen seemed about to agree, but stopped as he walked towards the stairs. 'There's another thing, Gus. I've been thinking about it all evening. How sure are you about this idea that Michelle's father could have murdered Gabriel?'

'I'm not *sure* at all. It's just plausible if he's still around.'

'But it would mean he must have found out about what was going on. He'd have to have seen them. Right?'

'Could be,' Maltravers agreed. 'That's how Flyte found out.'

'But not everybody peers around at night through a telescope.'

'No . . . so what are you saying?'

'That it could be someone who lives where they can see into the churchyard.'

'That's possible . . . although they could just have been walking past late at night.' Maltravers's eyes narrowed. 'What's on your mind, Stephen?'

'I can see into the churchyard from our bedroom window.'

132

Maltravers laughed. 'Now you're getting paranoid. For Christ's sake, I'm not suspecting you.'

'Neither am I.' Suddenly he did not seem to want to say any more. 'Anyway, I'll see you tomorrow afternoon. Goodnight, Gus. Thanks for dinner.'

Maltravers nearly called him back as he realised what he meant, then remained downstairs for nearly an hour.

Chapter Thirteen

The taxi driver was frustrated over his fare to Medmelton. Tall, slender redheads with an indefinable presence accentuated by Gucci luggage and black leather boots beneath a man's-style battleship grey trenchcoat, wide collar turned up and belted tight at the waist, did not appear off the Bristol train at Exeter St David's that often. He adjusted his rear view mirror so that he could glance at her from time to time; her jewel-green eyes lit an elusively familiar face.

'On holiday?' he ventured.

'Only for a couple of days,' she replied. There were maddeningly half-recognisable tones in the voice as well. 'How far is it to Medmelton?'

'Should take about twenty minutes at this time of day ... you've not been here before, then?'

'I haven't been in Devon since I was a little girl.'

He was positive he hadn't seen her locally anyway. As he turned off the A38, he tried to work it out. She was somehow well known – not so famous as to be unmistakable, but triggering subconscious recognition. If he'd not actually met her, he must have seen her picture somewhere, in the papers or on television ... television. Of course. *EastEnders? Coronation Street? Emmerdale Farm? Casualty? Bread?* He tried to remember if the voice had sounded American, opening up glamorous possibilities of *Dallas, Dynasty, The Colbys* or *Twin Peaks.* Even *Miami Vice.* He had to know and the only way was to ask.

'I've seen you, haven't I? On the TV?'

She smiled at him through the mirror. 'Possibly.'

'Thought so. Don't tell me ... I'll get it in a minute.' He

frowned in concentration as they crested the hill and dropped towards the village. 'Have you been in that magazine? *Hello*?'

'They once did a piece on me.'

'My wife'd know then,' he said confidently. 'She reads it every week and . . . got it! You're the girl with Bob Monkhouse on that quiz programme. The one who brings the contestants on. He's always making jokes about you. What's he like, incidentally? You know, in private like. I can't stand him, but the wife thinks he's marvellous.'

'Bob Monkhouse? He's . . . a very nice guy.' The assessment was based on a casual chat lasting about two minutes at some long-forgotten party.

'Is he? Well, it's all an act on the telly, innit? I tell you one thing, though. I know you're not as dumb as you seem. Not now I've met you.' Momentarily he returned his attention to his job. 'Where exactly is it you're going?'

'By the church will be fine.'

'Right you are.' As the cab stopped, he took a notebook off the front passenger seat. 'Call it seven quid . . . and an autograph? The wife'll be over the moon when I tell her.'

'Of course.' Tess accepted the notebook. 'What's her name?'

'Betty. Betty Dobbs. And mine's Harry.'

Tess hesitated for a moment, then wrote, 'With love to Betty and Harry. Keep watching,' followed by an over-florid version of her signature and several kisses. She passed the book back, and as she took out her purse to pay him the driver gazed at it as though she had given him the crown jewels.

'We'll be watching out for you next week,' he promised.

'You do that.' Tess handed him the fare and waited while he leapt out and opened the door then took her case from the boot. 'And I'll tell Bob Monkhouse he's got a big fan in Betty.'

'You won't say what I said about him, will you?' The driver sounded anxious, as though worried by an imperfect knowledge of the laws of slander.

'I'll leave that out. Thank you. 'Bye.'

She waved as he turned round and drove away, clutching a vicarious and completely mistaken touch of glamour from a tacky game show, ignorant of a string of acting credits and two

Bafta nominations. Such was fame. Picking up her case, she walked alongside the churchyard wall looking at the Lazarus Tree and recalling Maltravers's strange stories of what had been happening there. When she reached Dymlight Cottage, the front door was partly open and she stepped straight in.

'Hello,' she called. 'Anybody home?'

Maltravers appeared from the kitchen. 'Hi. Welcome back to Medmelton. It's all right, nobody else is here.' He crossed the room and kissed her. 'I didn't say anything about a birthmark. I had to take that on board in a hurry last night.'

'Creative input,' she told him. 'I thought it was rather clever. I wanted to make absolutely sure they remembered me.'

'The eyes would have done that. At least you remembered to wear the lens in the right one. Medmelton eyes reversed would certainly have been commented on. Incidentally, do you think anyone saw your car?'

'Possibly, but it was hired anyway. And what are they going to do if they did? Try and trace me through it?'

'Some of them are probably capable of trying, but we needn't worry about it . . . and did you meet Michelle?'

'Of course I did. Why do you ask?'

'She says you didn't. Claims she was out for part of the evening.'

'Well, she was in when I arrived.' Tess looked uncomfortable. 'And I scared her, Gus. I hope you know what you're doing.'

'We'll find out.' He picked up her suitcase. 'Let's get you settled in and you can tell me the details.'

Half an hour later, Tess stared into her tea as they sat at the kitchen table while Maltravers explained what had happened since they spoke on the telephone.

'So assuming Alex Kerr's right – and it's a persuasive suggestion – Mildred Thomson could be behind the churchyard games,' he concluded. 'Anyway, fill me in on last night.'

Tess sighed slightly, recalling something that troubled her. 'It was . . . I don't know. Disturbing. She looked puzzled when she opened the door. There was enough light for her to see my eyes. I'd polished your script a bit. I called her by her name, which obviously startled her, but when I said that what she was doing by the Lazarus Tree was very dangerous, she looked terrified. Then she tried the aggressive teenager bit. Who was I? Where did I come from? She even tried denying knowing what I was talking about, but I slapped her down. What really got to her was when I said I knew about Patrick Gabriel.'

'Just "about" him?' Maltravers interrupted.

'Of course.' The question annoyed her. 'I didn't start ad-libbing, for God's sake, throwing out some of your wild guesses. Anyway, she looked very apprehensive after that and asked what I wanted. I spelt out your scenario. In the churchyard tonight – well, tomorrow morning strictly speaking. One o'clock. With whoever had put her up to it. I felt absolutely stupid saying that. It's way over the top.'

'Yes it is,' he agreed. 'But it's the best way I can think of to guarantee results. Whoever's playing games with Michelle – possibly Mildred, but it could be someone else for all we know – has almost certainly got some dramatic kink to their person-ality. If you've convinced Michelle, and I'm pretty sure you did, she's going to pass it on. In fact she probably did go out last night after you left to talk to them. They daren't not turn up.'

'And what's going to happen?'

'At least I should be able to stamp very hard on this witchcraft crap, but whether it's going to throw any light on who murdered Patrick Gabriel – and why – God alone knows.'

The Medmelton telephones were busy again. Still alert for any-thing that might have even the remotest connection with Maltra-vers, Peggy Travis had kept faithful watch from her cottage. It was much more interesting than the endless saga of *The Archers* or anything provided by Mills and Boon paperbacks from the mobile library. The arrival of a taxi had been unusual enough; an unknown woman getting out of it and heading towards Dym-light Cottage was spectacular. Brief observation was duly ampli-fied for the satisfaction of all concerned.

'Very hard face. Tell you who she reminded me of. Greta Garbo. Cold. And she was wearing one of those coats like in those spy films. Red hair . . . quite tall . . . walked as if she owned the place . . . wouldn't like to be alone in a room with her for very long. Of course, it's the women who are the worst, isn't it? Stands to reason. They've got to show they're tougher than the men, haven't they? Do you think she's his boss? Come to check on how he's getting on? He'll be in for a right tongue-lashing if he can't come up with anything. What's he been doing? Well, I was out for a while yesterday morning, but Evelyn said she thought she saw him with Sally Baker in her car. Couldn't be certain, because she only got a glimpse. And her husband was in the Foreign Office, wasn't he? I know it's years since, but . . . well, it makes you think.'

Maltravers was providing the Medmelton rumour factory with raw material that would last for years.

In his study, Bernard Quex stared into space, pen motionless over his notepad. He had written, 'Idolatry? 2 Kings. 14:23–9? Gifts for God? Spikenard. Solomon, Mark?? Forgiveness? John, 8:7.' Having totally embraced the Bible as an incorrigible source of wisdom and truth, texts to support sermons spilled out without conscious effort, chapter and verse coming automatically as he considered possible themes. So 'Forgiveness' had instinctively produced the woman taken in adultery – and the comfort of Holy Writ had become chill reality which was increasingly difficult to keep at a distance. Forgiveness presumed some previous sin. Possibly derived from the Latin *sons*, meaning guilty, but in a Biblical sense failing to meet God's standards. A weakness. An abomination. A blasphemy. Academic interpretations held off the shame for a while, but then he could no longer close his mind to it. And still phrases of his belief came. He had uncovered her nakedness, he was a fornicator, they had known each other.

No, none of that. He had seduced another man's wife, taken her to bed and – Quex had to make his mind form the blunt words – he had . . . say it, *say* it! Had *fucked* her! Agonisingly, he forced himself to recognise what he had done – what he was still doing – by deliberately defining it in coarseness, wallowing in filth that it might make him clean. It became a strangely controlled, almost clinical, process, human passion reduced to basic carnality. When he finished, he was quivering.

And his hair shirt of guilt brought its perverse comfort again.

I am a sinner, Lord, and confess my sin. From You no secrets of the heart may be hid. 'If Thou, Lord, shouldest mark iniquities, O Lord who shall stand?' But Ursula was coming that afternoon and his cry would be the eternal excuse of Adam. The woman tempted me. Blame her. Forgive me. Forgive me all my trespasses. I have broken Thy commandments. But I confess. To You.

Ursula Dean played with impossible dreams. He would have to leave the church of course, but they could move away. Far away. To another country where anonymity would protect them. She knew Bernard had money of his own left by his parents and the law could make Ewan pay her at least half the value of their house. It would be dreadful for a while; the disgrace for Bernard, Ewan's fury, her mother's shame. But then it would be wonderful. She clung to the pleasures of imagination. Years ago, she'd been to Canada, staying with friends within sight of the clean beauty of the Rockies. It had all been so *big*, full of the empty spaces of sparkling mornings and night skies framed for giants. She would be able to ride again, turning in her saddle to see the man she loved beside her, then galloping away, laughing as he chased her. And they would ride to the lake in the mountains where it would seem as though they were the only people in the entire world and throw themselves on the grass and . . .

And the room suddenly closed in on her and the image of high prairies became suffocating Devon hills that trapped them. And this afternoon would be furtive, guilty love-making in Bernard's bedroom made claustrophobic by ancient furniture and the smell of dust. And afterwards, Bernard would pray.

Gilbert Flyte was angry. Maltravers had tricked him – there was no other word for it – had tricked him into making a fool of himself. And now he had a weapon to hold over him. An incipient bully without even a bully's sham courage, Flyte exercised authority with small-minded callousness; when threatened by authority, his resentment turned to fear and hatred. What made it more intolerable was that Maltravers had never had authority, he had only pretended, and now he had power without any right to it. Power over Gilbert Flyte. Power that could expose him. Suppose he brought the police in? Flyte knew he would not be able to withstand the agony of lying to them again; he would blurt everything out. And there was no escape. Whatever happened, Maltravers would remain a permanent threat. Everything Flyte valued in life – reputation, security, self-esteem, the success that he was certain his biography of Nelson would bring – could be brought down in ruins at any moment by one despicable man. As long as Maltravers lived, Gilbert Flyte would know no peace. As long as he lived . . . that way lay dreams of succulent satisfaction, fantasies of deputy bank manager become not frightened, desperate killer, but cold, deliberate assassin. So terrifyingly impossible – but so terribly comforting and tempting.

'What time do you think you'll be back?' Stephen asked.

'Don't wait up,' Maltravers advised. 'Tess was at school with the wife of the couple we're going to see, so it'll be impossible to prise them apart. You'd better let us have a key.'

'No need. We'll leave the door unlocked.'

'Will it be safe?'

'People round here often do it when they go out.' Stephen smiled sourly. 'Whatever else happens in Medmelton, we don't suffer from petty crime.'

'Lucky you. We'll come in quietly.'

'Where did you say this couple live?'

'Somewhere past Plymouth, across the border in Cornwall.'

'Remember there's a toll on the bridge when you come back over the Tamar. Anyway, see you when I get back from school tomorrow. I imagine you'll want to lie in in the morning.'

Fifteen minutes later, Maltravers reached the end of the Medmelton lane and turned left along the A38.

'Where are we meeting Sally Baker?' Tess asked.

'Pub at Buckfastleigh where I had lunch the other day. We'll be able to eat there as well.'

'Isn't it a bit close? If someone from Medmelton walks in and sees you together, it'll be round the place like wildfire.'

'It's not likely. Everyone sticks to their own local and I don't think my reputation has stretched outside Medmelton.'

Sally Baker was not there when they arrived, but walked in just as they had finished their meal. Maltravers was intrigued with how she and Tess subtly assessed each other, each slightly defensive. When he went to the bar for more drinks, he deliberately let other customers be served before him so that he could leave them alone for a few minutes. Certain questions and answers would only be possible in his absence.

'We've been trying to decide whether you're quite mad or very clever,' Sally announced as he returned to the table.

'And what's the verdict?'

'The jury's still out,' Tess said drily.

'If they say guilty, I shall plead insanity. There seems to be a lot of it about.' He glanced at his watch. 'However, further evidence should be forthcoming in about four hours. In the meantime, let's look at what we've got.'

He rested his elbows on the table, put his palms together and tapped his lips for a moment. 'Whatever else happens, tonight should crack this witchcraft nonsense. I'll lay money that Michelle will be there, with a confident side bet on her turning up with Mildred Thomson. But will it take us any nearer finding Gabriel's murderer?'

'It might take us right there,' Sally told him. 'It's got to be a possibility that it was Mildred.' She nodded towards Tess. 'I trust you can look after this lady.'

'She can do that herself,' Maltravers replied. 'In any case, killing a man who was probably fairly drunk when he wasn't expecting it is very different from taking on a young sober woman – easy on the Scotch, darling – who's on her guard. In any case, I can't see any reason why Mildred should have wanted to murder him.'

'There's an awful lot we can't see,' Sally reminded him. 'Once Gabriel and Mildred got to know each other, Heaven alone knows what they might have got up to.'

'True,' Maltravers acknowledged. 'But he was hardly here long enough for them seriously to fall out.'

'No, but if he got to know she was playing witchcraft with Michelle – or even some other local kids – he could have threatened to tell,' Sally suggested.

'The hell he would,' Maltravers said with conviction. 'He'd have got involved up to his ears. It's exactly the sort of thing that would have appealed to him. Just remember that he was a marvellous poet and a lousy human being.'

'So we're left with the suggestion that it was Michelle's father . . .' Sally began, then stopped when she saw the reaction on their faces. 'Aren't we?'

'Yes, but . . .' Maltravers looked uneasy. 'I've told Tess about this. After we got back from the Raven last night and I'd gone through the pantomime of being mystified by the woman visitor, Stephen said something. He didn't come right out with it, but his argument was that if it had been her father, he could have found out by seeing them. That meant he could live in a cottage with a view of the churchyard – like Dymlight has. And that frightened him.'

'Frightened him?' Sally frowned. 'Why?'

'He didn't say it, but it means that Veronica could have seen.' Maltravers took a long time over lighting a cigarette. 'It's the obvious converse of the father theory. It hadn't occurred to me, but Stephen saw it. Think about it. Veronica has an ultra-controlled personality. Whatever needs doing, she does it, no matter how difficult. She's protected Michelle's father's identity for all these years, so she's quite capable of protecting Michelle. If she'd been sneaking out at night to meet Gabriel, Veronica could have heard her – and seen them. According to Flyte's story, the figure he saw could have been a man or a woman and Gabriel was killed with one slash across the throat. Knock it down if you can.'

'I didn't like this one little bit when Gus told me,' Tess put in. 'But I hardly know Veronica and what she might be capable of.'

'I do.' Sally sighed then remained silent for a few moments, sliding her fingers up and down the stem of her wine glass. 'My mother once told me a story about Veronica when she was a little girl. She had a kitten and there was something wrong with it. The vet said it would have to be put down. Veronica asked to keep it for one more night. In the morning, her mother found it dead by her bed. Veronica had suffocated it herself because she didn't want the vet to do it.'

She looked at the unease in their faces. 'She was four years old at the time. When she was asked why, she said it was because she loved it.'

'Ouch,' Tess said quietly.

'Ouch indeed,' Sally repeated, then turned to Maltravers. 'Stephen's right. It could have been her.'

Chapter Fourteen

Frustrated and increasingly fearful, Mildred Thomson stared at the crawling spearhead hands of the clock on the sideboard. More than another hour to wait. Was Michelle lying about this visitor? It did not seem likely. The girl had been terrified when she had dashed into the house the previous evening, face pale, words spluttering out in panic. She had not recognised the woman; she was positive it was no one she knew. But vivid Medmelton eyes had been clearly visible in the light from the living room. Mildred had pressed for more details. How tall? About as tall as Mum. Colour of hair? Couldn't see, she was wearing a headscarf. Voice? Did she sound local? Yes . . . no . . . perhaps. Michelle was not sure. She was too scared to think about things like that. What *exactly* had the woman said? That she knew what was happening in the churchyard . . . that it was very serious . . . that Michelle had to be there with the person who was making her do it at the time the woman said. If not, there would be a great deal of trouble. Had Michelle asked her name? No. She was so . . . so frightening. She said she knew about Patrick Gabriel!

Michelle had started to weep with terror, begging Mildred to come with her. They daren't not go. The woman would speak to Mum if they didn't. If they went, at least they might be able to keep it quiet. They *had* to keep it quiet. For both their sakes. Mildred had sharply told her to pull herself together and had sat thinking while the girl sobbed and sniffed softly.

'Do you know who she is?' Michelle had finally asked. It was as if she was grasping at a frantic hope that it had been some sort of test devised by Mildred.

'No. But I have to talk to her.'

As the clock dropped slow seconds through the room, Mildred Thomson wracked her brains. During the day, customers had told her about the strange woman's appearance at the Raven. Controlling her reaction, she had casually gathered what information she could. Rumour had confused the picture, but the Medmelton eyes and the partly visible birthmark were consistent. The best guess put her in her late twenties. Mildred could remember no girl from the village with such a disfigurement, so she had not been born here, but possibly one of her parents had. That made it impossible to identify her; countless people had moved away over the years. But how did she know about Michelle and the churchyard? If she'd been in the village before last night, surely word would have reached the stores. She had appeared out of nowhere, knowing things impossible for her to know. Where from? Why? What did she want? Who *was* she? There was a whirring sound, then the clock's chime marked a quarter to midnight. Only another hour.

Sally Baker gave a complimentary nod as Tess reappeared from upstairs. Long bright russet hair which had reached far down her back earlier in the evening had been wound into a tight bun covered with a cream silk scarf, a dull red-purple smear creeping on to her right cheek from one edge of it. The wide collar of the grey raincoat was turned up like wings, half folded round her head. Sally crossed the room and looked at her carefully; the right eye was now chestnut brown, in striking contrast to the green of the left.

'Isn't the lens uncomfortable?' she asked.

'A bit, but . . .' Tess grinned unexpectedly. 'Can you keep a secret? I wear them all the time.'

'Blind as a bat if she takes them out,' Maltravers commented.

'I'm not,' Tess contradicted. 'I just don't like wearing glasses.'

'"Vanity of vanities, and everything is vanity". I can do that in Latin as well if you want.'

'Stop showing off,' Tess told him. 'And isn't it interesting that suddenly we're making jokes?'

'Nervous laughter,' Sally said. 'It's hardly surprising. Do we leave now? There's still an hour to go and it's only ten minutes' walk.'

'I think it's better to be early,' Maltravers said. 'We want to get there without being seen as well.'

'Nobody's likely to be around at this time of night and it's starting to rain,' Sally assured him. 'Hang on a minute and I'll get the torch.'

The rain had settled into a persistent thin drizzle as they left Sally's cottage. The country silence Maltravers had noticed on his first night was wrapped in an all-embracing cloak of black, unfamiliar and disorienting to those who unconsciously lived within permanent reach of artificial lighting. From the top of the hill, Medmelton was virtually invisible, then cottages on its outskirts appeared uncertainly in the gloom, silent and still as they walked down. By the time they reached the green, their eyes had adjusted to what minimal illumination there was. Sally opened the lychgate very slowly, stopping when it was just wide enough for them to pass through.

'It squeaks,' she whispered.

The porch of St Leonard's seemed to hold an extra darkness of its own and the churchyard suddenly appeared comparatively light. Gravestones stood like random sentinels; drizzle gathered on the leaves of heavy yews, copper beech and the Lazarus Tree, dripping with infinite softness. At twenty to one, Tess went to stand by the tree, tall, black-booted, cloaked in her raincoat. As they waited, Maltravers silently took the torch from Sally Baker's hand, then they stiffened as the lychgate creaked. Tess turned towards the sound, and two figures, anonymous as silhouettes, appeared. She did not speak as they stopped on the edge of the path, hesitant as inquiring animals smelling danger.

'Thank you for coming.' Tess's voice was very low, but still carried clearly through the night. 'It's saved a lot of trouble.'

Mildred cleared her throat. 'Who are you?'

'My name isn't important.'

Maltravers and Sally instinctively moved back further into their hiding place as Mildred switched on a torch, pointing it straight at Tess's face. She responded by deliberately stepping forward and the beam flickered nervously.

'See? You don't recognise me, do you?'

There was a moment's pause, then Mildred Thomson shook her head. 'No. But I can see you're from here. What do you want?'

'First of all, I want some answers. It's all right, Michelle. There's nothing to be afraid of. Just tell me how this all began.'

'All what began?' Mildred Thomson snapped.

'I'm talking to Michelle,' Tess told her sharply. 'You'll get your chance in a moment. Michelle?'

'I don't know what you're talking about.' The aggressive, egotistical teenager was a very frightened little girl.

'Yes, you do,' Tess said with a coaxing softness. 'Shall I say it for you? After Patrick Gabriel died, Mildred told you there was a way in which he might be brought back. She gave you one of Ralph the Talespinner's stories to read, didn't she? About a woman called Mary of Medmelton and a man she was in love with. Why didn't you just laugh at her, Michelle? You're too grown up for fairy stories. Why did you believe her?'

The girl lowered her head and scuffed the toe of her shoe in the gravel of the path. 'I didn't believe her. I wanted to in a way, but I knew it was stupid. I just did it because . . . because it helped.'

'Helped? In what way?'

'Because . . . no.' Sulky defiance came to her defence. 'If you're so clever, you tell me.'

'I know a lot, Michelle. I know that you're in very serious trouble. But I don't know everything.'

'Then I'm not going to tell you.'

'But you've got to tell me. Because if you don't, I'm going to have to talk to the police.'

'And what can they do?' There was a trace of rebellious contempt at the threat of authority.

'Oh, stop being stupid!' Tess was suddenly impatient. 'Do you think they've forgotten about the murder and that it will all just go away? They're going to want to know about you and Patrick Gabriel . . . including who killed him.'

Her voice had barely risen, but its icy savagery stung the girl. She shook her head violently.

'I don't know!' she cried. 'Stop it! I didn't see anybody! I just found him! He was dead!' In the porch, Maltravers and Sally Baker stopped breathing.

'Found him?' Tess sounded appalled, then was instantly sympathy and understanding. 'Christ, darling, that must have been awful.'

She stepped forward, but Michelle backed away in alarm. 'It's all right. You're quite safe. It's me, Tess.' The girl peered at her in the gloom, then sobbed with shock and relief. Tess put her arm round her, then glanced at Mildred Thomson. 'What the hell have you been doing to this kid?'

The woman looked down, torch beam shining on the ground. 'Nothing she didn't want.'

'Which you put her up to,' Tess said bitterly. 'She was scared and grief-stricken and you bloody well played games with her.'

'She said she wanted him back,' the woman muttered. 'To talk to him.'

'And instead of listening to her, instead of telling her parents, you fed her crap. She needed help and you told her ghost stories.' Still holding Michelle, Tess stepped back towards the Lazarus Tree. 'Do you really believe what you told her? Because if you do, you are *sick*!'

'There are things you don't know, but you should.' There was angry excitement in Mildred Thomson's voice. 'You've got the power!'

'What power, you . . .' Tess stumbled in disbelief, '. . . you stupid bitch! There is no power.'

'Of course there is. You've got the eyes!'

'Sod the bloody eyes! This brown one's a contact lens and even if it was real, it wouldn't mean anything!'

'What do you mean?' The torch beam flashed back at her face. 'Who are you? What are you playing at?'

'Turn that thing off,' Tess ordered. 'We're not playing. We . . .'

'We?' The question cracked like a whip. 'What do you mean, we?'

Inside the porch Maltravers touched Sally Baker's hand. 'Stay here,' he breathed, then stepped outside. 'She means me too, Mildred.'

As the woman whirled round, he switched on Sally Baker's torch and the two beams crossed like lances. Raising her head from Tess's shoulder, Michelle recognised him and gave a gasp of shock.

'What's going on?' Startled by the sudden light on her face, Mildred Thomson backed away, staring urgently from Maltravers to Tess. 'I've not done anything wrong. I've not broken any laws.'

'Yes you have,' Maltravers contradicted. 'Withholding evidence for a start. You knew that Michelle found Patrick Gabriel's body and didn't tell the police. There may be a few other things as well, but that's up to them to sort out.'

'She never told me she found the body.' The denial came out too quickly. 'She just said . . . just said that she wanted to . . . wanted to ask the cards about him.'

'What cards?'

'The . . . you wouldn't understand.'

'I might, but we won't bother about that. What did she want to ask them?'

'She didn't say. She . . . she wouldn't tell me everything. I didn't want to do it, but she insisted. I didn't think there was any harm in it.'

Michelle suddenly clung very tightly to Tess, burying her face in the raincoat's damp fabric.

'No!' she sobbed. 'No, no, no, no, no!'

'It's all right,' Tess murmured soothingly as she stroked her hair. 'We know she's lying.'

'And that's what you're going to tell the police, is it?' Maltravers asked caustically. 'That you let a terrified child who'd found a murdered man talk you into playing insane superstitious games? That you told her to come here and secretly put things under the Lazarus Tree, that you said she had to recite the burial service backwards – oh, yes, I know about that as well – and that this has been going on for months? And you never wanted

149

to do it, but you didn't think there was any harm in it. You're brilliant at self-deception, Mildred.'

'It was her idea.' Michelle did not raise her head from Tess's shoulder and the resentful words were muffled. 'It was all her idea.'

'Of course it was,' Maltravers said. 'And it was very wicked of her.'

Mildred Thomson backed away further. In the silence, they could hear her panting with panic.

'Who sent you?' she demanded. 'Where are you from?'

'Nobody sent us,' Maltravers replied impatiently. 'I know everybody's been making hysterical guesses about who I am and why I'm here, but I'm just a friend of Stephen and Veronica's, nothing else.'

'But you've been asking questions,' the woman said accusingly.

'Yes, I have,' he agreed. 'And now I have some answers. Not all of them yet, but enough to be going on with.'

'If you're not from the police, I'm not saying any more.' She pointed the torch beam at Michelle, then flicked it away again. 'She's crazy, that one. They always are when the eyes are reversed. Nobody's going to believe her.' Michelle moaned in Tess's arms.

'My God, you really are vile.' Maltravers shone his torch straight at Mildred Thomson's face again, then shook himself in disgust. 'Just get the hell out of here – and leave this girl alone from now on. If I want to hear from you again, I'll bang on your bloody cauldron.'

Angry, defiant and frightened, she sneered and Tess closed her eyes as though in pain. 'Bloody off-comers with your fancy London ways. You don't belong here. I'm going all right, but not because you tell me to. This is my village and nobody tells me what to do. Go and tell the police for all I care. They can't touch me.'

Maltravers sighed as she clumped away in the dripping darkness. The lychgate squeaked again, then her footsteps faded.

'At least she didn't spit,' he muttered to himself, then went over to Tess and Michelle, putting his own arm around the sobbing girl. 'Come on, we've got to talk. Let's go into the porch out of the rain. There's someone else there, but it's all right. She's on your side as well.'

Little inarticulate noises choking from her throat, Michelle let them lead her into the porch. When she saw Sally Baker, she looked blank, beyond any more reaction. Tess sat her down on the stone seat and put a protecting arm round her again.

'You'll be in bed soon,' she promised. 'Come on, you can hack it. Just tell us everything that happened.'

The girl shook her head feebly. 'I can't.'

'Yes, you can,' Tess insisted gently. 'I'll tell you what. We'll tell you what we think and you say when we're wrong. All right? Well, that's what we'll do anyway . . . Patrick Gabriel was your lover, wasn't he?'

She tightened her grip as the girl instantly tried to pull away. 'No! That's not what we want to talk about. It doesn't matter. You used to meet him by the Lazarus Tree, didn't you?' Unexpectedly she laughed. 'Oh, you silly girl. Believe me, darling, there are millions of better fish in the sea. I bet he told you he was going to take you away to live in London with him, didn't he?'

Michelle gave a tiny nod. 'He promised,' she whispered.

'Of course he did. He'd promise anything, that one. Start getting angry at him. He used you and . . .'

'He said he loved me.'

'Oh, they always say that,' Tess told her. 'So you've learnt something, haven't you? Remember it. How long did it go on for?'

'Four or five weeks – but not every night! I know how many times we . . . it's in my diary . . . I can't remember exactly, but it must have been about . . .'

'We don't need the details,' Tess interrupted. 'It's happened and it's over and done with . . . did you take precautions?'

'He said there was no need. He'd had an operation.'

Tess groaned and took hold of her by the shoulders, turning her face towards herself. 'Now listen to me. *Never* believe that. You got away with it this time, but you might not be so lucky again.' She smiled apologetically, then cuddled her. 'Sorry. I didn't mean to sound cross. But *please* be careful in future.'

As the girl gave a nervous smile and nodded, Maltravers felt that Tess's commonsense talk had managed to calm her down sufficiently. He moved forward and was about to speak, when Sally Baker touched his arm to stop him before crouching down and taking hold of Michelle's hand.

'Look at me, Michelle,' she urged softly. 'That's it. Now come on. You hardly know Gus and Tess, but you've known me a long time and there's something very important we have to talk about. Just now you said that you found Patrick Gabriel. It was going to be one of your arranged meetings, was it? Was that a yes? All right, now tell us everything you can remember.'

There was a very long silence before she spoke. 'I just found him. I thought at first he'd gone to sleep, then I saw . . . I thought he was wearing a red scarf, but when I touched it . . .' She shuddered.

'What did you do?' Sally asked.

'I think . . . no, I didn't faint, but I went very dizzy and the next thing I was running back to the cottage. I could hardly see, I was crying so much. I went to my room and locked the door and . . . I jumped into bed and pulled the duvet right over me. I was so scared.'

'Of course you were.' Sally squeezed her hand. 'Why didn't you tell someone?'

'I couldn't!' she protested. 'They'd have wanted to know what I was doing out at that time of night. They might have thought I did it!'

'Michelle, nobody would have thought that! Why should they?'

'I'd still have had to explain why I was there and it would all have come out about me and Patrick and what we'd done.' She gulped and sobbed again. 'I went to sleep for a bit and by the morning someone else had found him and it was all . . . all panicky. There were police all over the place. I remember praying for Steve to take me to school so I could get away from it. I had to make myself ask him about it in the car, because I knew it would seem wrong if I didn't. He didn't say very much – I think he was trying to protect me in a way and I knew he was being kind, but I wanted to know what the police were doing. I had to know.

'It was awful at school because everyone had heard and kept asking me questions. The teachers kept asking me if I was all right and I had to bottle it all up inside me.' Tears were spilling from brown and green eyes as the words came faster. 'And if you keep something like that inside, it becomes . . . I don't know . . . it sort of hardens, like a shell or something and you can hide inside it and nobody can get at you. I remember acting stupid, laughing at silly things. At break time, I even played chase and I never did that because it was for little kids.'

She dropped her head. 'And I wanted to be little again.'

Sally Baker straightened up and when she turned to face Maltravers she looked dreadful.

'You do it now,' she whispered. 'I can't any more.'

Maltravers nodded understandingly then leant forward, arms resting on his knees.

'And you've kept it bottled up all this time? I wish I was as brave as you. Anyway, you've told us now and it'll soon be over. Just a couple more questions and then we'll get you home. How did you and Patrick arrange your meetings? You said it wasn't every night.'

She shrugged. 'They just happened. We'd just meet like it was casual and decide. Sometimes I wanted to, but he didn't. We always made it for just after midnight because I knew Mum and Steve would be asleep by then. They always go to bed early.'

'And why by the Lazarus Tree?' Maltravers asked. 'You could have gone to his cottage.'

'That was his idea. It was something to do with the story – you know, about the girl waiting under it. I didn't really understand, but he said it tied in with the poem he was writing and . . . God, I feel so stupid!'

'Hold on to that,' Maltravers told her. 'You're finding your temper. Anyway, the important thing is the night it happened. Now we realise how awful it was for you, but just think about it for a moment. When you went out – before you found him – was there anything at all you can remember?'

'No,' she insisted. 'I was hurrying because it was nearly half past midnight and I thought Patrick might have gone. Uncle Ewan and Auntie Ursula had come round and they stayed late. I had to wait until I was certain Mum and Steve were asleep. I didn't see anyone or hear anything or . . . it was a summer night, but very dark. I've thought and thought about it, but I just went out and it was quiet and I climbed over the wall and . . .'

'All right.' Maltravers stopped her continuing. 'You've told us the rest. Come on, let's get you home.'

'What are you going to do?' she asked as he stood up.

'Nothing at the moment,' he replied. 'Except to repeat one thing that you've just learnt. Mildred Thomson is very bad news. Right?'

'I know that now – it was stupid, but I . . .' She shook her head. 'I can't explain it . . . but aren't you going to have to tell Mum?'

Maltravers had to look away. 'I can't promise, but if we can avoid it, we will. All right? In the meantime, just hang on in there. We may need to talk to you again, but for the time being all this is just between the four of us. Now home. If Mum or Steve hear anything, they'll assume it's just us coming back. Go with Tess and I'll catch you up.'

He and Sally Baker remained in the porch, watching them walk towards the lychgate with their arms round each other. Michelle was wearily resting her head against Tess.

'What a bloody mess,' Sally murmured.

'Ain't that the truth?' Maltravers lit a cigarette. 'I don't see how we've got much further on the murder, but we've stamped on Medmelton's secret, black and midnight hag. Jesus, she should be locked up. Do you think she's been doing this sort of thing with any other kids?'

'I have a horrible feeling it's possible,' Sally said. 'But leave that with me. She doesn't know I was here tonight, so I can do things without her realising.'

'I'm sure you'll sort it,' Maltravers acknowledged. 'In the meantime, we'd better have another talk tomorrow. Come on, I'll see you home.'

'I can manage. Medmelton's safe enough.'

'Is it?'

'Nobody stops me walking through my village. Goodnight, Gus.'

After she left, Maltravers stared at the Lazarus Tree as he finished his cigarette and the depth of Mildred Thomson's malevolence began to sink in. She ran the local shop, everyone knew her, she was an institution in a secluded Devon village. When she died, they would pack the church for her funeral service, full of stories about her gossip and her eccentricities. Bernard Quex would recall how she had been a part of so many lives, how they would miss her, how Medmelton would never be the same again. Somebody else would take over the stores, but for years people would say, 'It's not like it was in Mildred's day.' They'd never know and perhaps they wouldn't want to . . . the glowing cigarette end spun into the darkness and he walked back to Dymlight Cottage.

The front door was still unlocked as he let himself in and went quietly upstairs. Tess was sitting in front of the dressing table, bowed head over cupped hand as she removed the brown contact lens.

'How is she?' he asked.

'She was almost asleep in my arms. Reaction. I just took her shoes off and put her into bed.' She raised her face and looked at him through the mirror. 'So what do we do now?'

He shrugged. 'Sleep on it – if we can – and see if the morning brings any ideas. I'll tell Stephen what's happened when he gets back tomorrow afternoon. At least we've sorted out one of his worries.'

'But not the worst one.'

'I'm afraid not.'

Half an hour later, Maltravers turned off the bedside light and they lay in the darkness holding hands.

'There's one suggestion I can't shake off,' Tess said. 'It's probably because all I can see at the moment is that goddamned woman's face. Do you think she could have murdered Gabriel? She looks capable of it.'

'But why? We'll see what Sally thinks . . . and we'll ask her friend Mr Kerr.'

'Why him?'

'Because Mr Kerr is a very clever man.' He squeezed her hand. 'It's late. Sleep.'

Tess closed her eyes, forcing her mind on to any prosaic thing that would drive out hideous images. Helen's birthday next week . . . organise a present . . . ring her agent about that film role, very small but should pay well . . . write that damned letter to the States . . . remind Gus about getting the car serviced . . . what would Helen like? . . . fix up a dinner party with Donna and Jeremy . . . book tickets for . . .

Lying awake beside her, Maltravers could see only the image of the Lazarus Tree as it would look from Stephen and Veronica's bedroom at the other end of the landing.

Chapter Fifteen

Michelle's body trembled and she gave a little cry. Fragments of a dream whirled in her half-conscious mind then fled like smoke suddenly blown away, fading images confused with the reality of what had happened in the churchyard. Patrick alive and kissing her as his features changed into Mildred's treacherous face; sweet chestnuts from the Lazarus Tree split open and running blood; Tess's fabricated Medmelton eyes blazing with accusation; Maltravers and Sally Baker rising from behind a gravestone. For a few seconds everything was real and nothing was real, then her alarm clock snapped her into complete wakefulness. She was still wearing her clothes. Uncertain as the vanished dream, she could half remember Tess supporting her as they walked back to the cottage, but after that there was nothing.

She sat up abruptly, fingers violently scrubbing her short hair as though to agitate her brain into action. She could rationalise it now. The stupidity with Mildred was over and apprehension at its exposure was mixed with relief. Maltravers was a disturbing figure, now knowing too much and in control. She hated that, but had to accept it and be ready to respond to what might happen. Ready to lie if necessary, to deny and adopt new masks.

During breakfast, Stephen made occasional conversation, Veronica was efficient and calm, Tess acted the polite guest and Maltravers went into detached writer's mode as he watched everyone else. An outsider would have seen four adults and a sulky teenager, half listening to Radio 4, going through the motions of starting another day. The meal finished, Tess insisted on doing the washing up, Stephen and Michelle left for school and Maltravers went into the front room with the morning paper. At nine, Veronica went to catch the bus into Exeter; a few minutes after she left, the telephone rang and Maltravers answered it.

'Good morning, Sally.'

'How's Michelle?'

'Coping. Went to sleep like a baby and seems to be in control of herself again this morning.'

'That's typical, but I'm not sure how complete that control is. She's toughing it out and it would be better if she cracked.'

'Perhaps she will.' Maltravers was painfully conscious of further agonies the girl might have to go through. 'Look, we have to talk . . . and I'd like your friend Alex Kerr there as well. Can you coax him out of his warren for coffee at your place?'

'He'll come if I ask him. But why?'

'First, because we've all got emotional hang-ups about this and need someone detached to bounce things off. Second, because I found him . . . very shrewd.' Maltravers paused and felt uncertainty in the hesitation from the other end of the line. 'Sally, some things are not my business. Both you and Alex have told me he worked for the Post Office and I'll go along with that . . . all right?'

He waited for her to break the silence. 'He said you were sharp.'

'And discreet,' he assured her. 'We'll see you in about half an hour.'

Tess frowned at him as he rang off. 'What was all that about this Alex Kerr?'

'There's a lot more to Mr Kerr than he cares to admit, but he has his reasons for keeping it quiet. However, dropping the hint that I realise it might let him be a little more direct in throwing out suggestions.'

'You mean you want him to come up with some explanation as to why it couldn't have been Veronica.'

'I want that very much. Because I still can't see why she might not have done it. And I don't like that.'

Head bowed and clasped hands resting on the altar rail, Bernard Quex knelt in the silence of St Leonard's. All the standard preliminaries had been uttered automatically – did he ever think about what he was saying any more? – and he had prayed for the good of his flock, his parish and his church, comfort for Jane Dawson in her illness and Harry Clark in his grief. For the souls of my mother and father and all those departed, for the guidance of those living, for the Queen and those who counsel her that they might have wisdom, for peace in the world. In the name of our Lord and Only Begotten Saviour, Jesus Christ. Amen.

And now he must pray for himself. Stooped supplicant shoulders rose and fell as he breathed very deeply. For strength in my weakness, Lord. For forgiveness of my sin. That You might weigh that which I have done well in Thy name and find I am not wanting. For recognition of my suffering. For help in my confusion, for absolution of my guilt. Of my guilt, that is so . . .

He sobbed violently. The image of Ursula Dean had invaded his mind, instantly bringing him face to face with the fever and irresistible craving of it all. Not once, not twice, but . . . too often, when once had been too many. And that afternoon she was coming to the Rectory again and they . . . he shuddered.

'Father, forgive me,' he whispered. 'For I know what I do and what I have done.'

'Is anything the matter, Mildred?'

'What? No, of course not. Why should there be?' Mildred Thomson glared defiantly as she slammed the half pound of smoked back bacon down on the counter. 'Is that all?'

'Oh . . . yes, I think so. How much altogether.'

'Four pounds seventeen. Thank *you*.' She snatched the note and flicked the change from the drawer of the till. 'Who's next? Are you going to look at those cabbages all day or are you going to buy one?'

'Somebody got out of bed the wrong side this morning,' a woman at the back of the shop muttered.

Mildred Thomson's behaviour was a confusion of fear and anger. Fear of the threatened destruction of a lifetime's reputation; anger at having been tricked and being now in danger from outsiders. In Medmelton which she had embraced as her world, sublimating abandoned hopes and desires in the security of her power, knowing that this place was hers, that she knew those who lived here and all the details of their lives. That she could play games with them, casually passing on just enough gossip she had heard from one to affect another. And she had become skilled at it, subtle in manipulation, secretly rejoicing over the petty jealousies and misunderstandings she created, endless revenge for years of real and imagined slights. Because she had remained the unimportant, disregarded woman who ran the village shop, unthinkingly accepted and trusted by them all. It had been compensation for all she could not have but had wanted so desperately. But suddenly she was no longer in control and . . .

'Not that one, Mildred. I never have that brand.'

'What?' She stared at the packet of soap powder she had taken from the shelf. For the first time in forty years she had made a mistake while putting an order together. It was strange how much such a little thing hurt, as though part of her self-esteem had been torn away.

Ewan Dean did not look up from the newspaper as the shop bell sounded; it was probably just another casual customer browsing around until they decided to buy nothing. It underlined how bad business was and if things didn't improve soon . . .

'Hello, Ewan.'

Now he took notice. 'I thought you were at work.'

'Not for another half hour.' Veronica stepped behind the counter. 'Any chance of a coffee?'

'The kettle's just boiled.' He stepped down off the high wooden stool and she followed him into the back of the shop. 'What brings you here?'

'Something happened the other night. We'd been out to dinner with Gus and when we got back Stephen heard some story in the pub about a woman calling at the cottage. Michelle said she didn't see her because she'd gone out, but she's lying.'

'You're sure of that?'

'I always know,' she said simply. 'What worries me is why.'

Her brother handed her a mug. 'Who was she? This woman.'

'Nobody knows – but she had Medmelton eyes and a birthmark on her face. I certainly can't place her. Nobody knows what she wanted either. She just went into the pub and asked where Dymlight Cottage was.'

'If she was from Medmelton, she should have known that.'

'Of course she should. I don't like it, Ewan.'

'It's not like you to get worried. What else is there?'

Veronica smiled thinly. 'We've always known each other so well, haven't we? Of course there's something else. Stephen didn't ask Gus down by chance and he's up to something. Haven't you heard? Medmelton's talking about nothing else.'

Dean shrugged. 'I've not been out for the past few days and Ursula hasn't mentioned anything. What's he up to?'

'Asking questions about Patrick Gabriel.'

'What? That all went quiet months ago. I'd forgotten about it.'

'I hadn't.'

Dean stepped forward and took her chin in his hands. 'Why not? It was nothing to do with you.'

Veronica pushed his hand down and turned her face away from him. 'Don't press me, Ewan. I need to talk.'

Alexander Kerr had taken the chair directly in front of the side window of Sally Baker's front room. As he listened, holding a white fluted cup and saucer, his head remained motionless as pencil-lead eyes flickered towards each of them in turn, but there was no other reaction until they had finished.

'So after these midnight dramas in the churchyard, you don't like what you've ended up with,' he remarked. 'Perhaps you shouldn't have started in the first place.'

'We didn't know what we'd end up with,' Maltravers said.

'And if you had, would you not have done anything?'

Maltravers sighed. 'I don't know. Possibly.'

'Well, it's too late now.' Kerr smiled sympathetically. 'However, let's see if there are other alternatives to Veronica killing her daughter's seducer – although that's probably slandering the dead. Michelle Dean is no innocent.'

'Do you think there are alternatives?' Maltravers asked.

'I suggest you think about them.' Kerr's tone prompted him.

'All right,' Maltravers agreed. 'Before we get on to specifics, let's look at the general. The only possible motive we've come up with for anyone killing Patrick Gabriel is that someone discovered what was going on between him and Michelle and cared enough about her to do something about it. That means . . .'

'Just a moment,' Kerr interrupted. 'You're using "cared" in the sense of loved. But Gilbert Flyte's admitted he saw them – and he might have "cared" in a different way.'

'What do you mean?' Maltravers asked.

'Gilbert Flyte is a little man with delusions that he's a big one. He bullies his wife, he's the type who'd be intolerable to work under and he convinces himself that one day he will be recognised as a great biographer. He is also sexually frustrated. Anyone who's seen his face whenever an attractive and preferably young woman walks into the Raven would know that.' Kerr sipped his coffee, then used the cup to gesture dismissively. 'I tend to notice how people behave. Put it down as a bored old man's hobby.'

'And what do you . . . deduce from your hobby in this case?'

'I normally don't bother with deductions, but . . .' Kerr paused. 'I think I might manage a plausible scenario. Flyte lusts after young women but they'll have nothing to do with him. He then sees a very young one giving herself to a much older man. That heightens his frustration to the point where it has to be satisfied by any means. So he kills Patrick Gabriel. He then tells Michelle he knows what she's been up to and unless she does the same for him . . . it's just a theory.' He sounded apologetic.

'And when he convinces himself that I'm about to arrest him, he blabs out part of the story and hopes that will be enough to avoid some very awkward questions,' Maltravers concluded. 'Yes, it's plausible.'

'No, it's not,' Sally said. 'Michelle would have told us last night.'

'Don't be dense, Sally.' There was disappointment in Kerr's reprimand. 'Michelle Dean is a liar. When you were with her in the churchyard, she admitted no more than she had to. You'd exposed her activities with Mildred Thomson and how they were linked to Gabriel. What she said may have been true – but did she tell you everything?'

'And if it was Flyte, there's no problem,' Maltravers added. 'He'll crack the moment the police start questioning him.'

'Don't grab hold of my theory just because it's more acceptable than what you've got,' Kerr warned. 'You don't have any proof.'

'People only blurt out conveniently comprehensive confessions in murder mysteries,' Maltravers commented. 'In real life, they defy you to prove it. And that could be a problem. Anyway, what else is there?'

'Michelle's father of course. That's plausible – but who is he?' Kerr turned to Sally Baker. 'Your connections with Medmelton are longer than any of ours. Suggestions?'

'I've thought a lot about that.' She stared into the remains of her coffee. 'There are three men still living here who were part of the group that Veronica belonged to in her teens, but I'm not aware that any of them was ever a boyfriend as such. Ewan was the protective older brother looking after his little sister. To be honest, I don't remember her having boyfriends.'

'Come on, Sally, she must have done,' Tess protested. 'I've got an older brother and he could be ridiculously jealous of anyone who took an interest in me, but I found plenty of ways round it. Any girl as attractive as Veronica would have had boyfriends.'

'I expect so,' Sally agreed. 'But I've never heard of anyone special – and Medmelton would have known about that.'

'Perhaps not in this case,' Maltravers pointed out. 'Veronica's very good at keeping secrets – she's passed that on to Michelle. But if one of them got her pregnant, why did she refuse to identify him? And still does . . . Alex?'

'Well . . .' Kerr gazed at the ceiling for a moment. 'As I understand it, Veronica and Ewan and their friends all belonged to the church youth group, social activities being somewhat restricted in these parts. That's always been run by Bernard Quex – who you now believe is having an affair with a married woman. So the question we might ask is did he start his philandering earlier?'

'We've already thought that,' Maltravers told him. 'And it would explain why Veronica never named him. But . . .'

'Just a minute,' Tess interrupted. 'Didn't Gilbert Flyte say that he saw the murderer walk off down the side of the church? Towards the back? Where the rectory is.'

'Yes,' Maltravers confirmed. 'But the cottage Patrick Gabriel rented is round there as well – and remember that after the murder all his notes were taken. Gabriel certainly told Stephen about the poem he was working on and he'd have told anyone else who took an interest. Love – sacred, profane, legal and illegal . . . like sex with a minor? If the killer was protecting Michelle – bringing us neatly back to the father theory – he'd have stolen the notes in case there was anything in them that could identify her.'

'Which could include Veronica,' Sally said sadly.

'I'm afraid it does . . . Help us out, Alex.'

'I don't know that I'm much use . . . but part of your reasoning is that Veronica could have seen them in the churchyard from Dymlight Cottage. She doesn't have an exclusive view. Flyte's admitted he saw them and anyone taking a late night walk in the summer might have done as well without them being aware of it. From my recollections of the activity, I seem to recall there are at least brief periods when one is . . . not concentrating on anything else.'

He turned to Sally. 'You say there are three men who grew up with Veronica still living in the village. A number of cottages in Medmelton have a view of the churchyard. Do they live in any of them?'

'One does – and the others could have been walking by.' She smiled at Maltravers. 'There *are* other options.'

'Including, of course, Mildred Thomson.' There was a silence while he drew on his cigarette. 'I just wish I could see a motive there.'

Kerr made a dubious noise in the back of his throat. 'After what she's been up to, I can appreciate you'd like that. But can you really make that dog run?'

'Possibly. If I was imaginative enough.'

'Oh, I think you should be imaginative.' Kerr's eyes had half closed and he was smiling slightly. 'But don't limit it to Mildred . . . Sally, is there any more of this excellent coffee?'

'Pardon? Yes, of course. I'll make some.'

'I'll come and help you.'

Maltravers remained in his chair for a moment, then went to the window overlooking the hill dropping into the village. A rising wind had made the day very clear and sunlight glinted off the gilded face of St Leonard's tower clock. He saw a woman leave Medmelton Stores and walk alongside the green then go through the gate of Gilbert Flyte's cottage. Looking towards the back of the church, the slate roof of the rectory was just visible above the trees. Tess came to stand next to him.

'What does he mean?' she asked. 'About being imaginative?'

'I don't know. He's crafty as a fox and he knows something – or has worked something out – but wants me to get there on my own. I should be flattered that he thinks I can do it.'

'Do you think he's trying to push you towards Stephen? That's why he won't say it.' She sighed. 'But he was the one who asked you here.'

'But Stephen's worked out that Veronica could have been the killer and wants to protect her. Is that it? Hell, we wanted Alex to talk us out of that. *Think*, dummy.'

He leant against the window sill, staring at the view without seeing it, mentally ransacking everything he knew. The drama had a small cast. Stephen and Veronica, Bernard Quex, Mildred Thomson, Gilbert Flyte . . . and the three men Sally had mentioned. But Medmelton was close-knit, jealous of its privacy, fiercely protective of its own. Even the police had been sent away empty-handed. And what about Michelle herself? Used by a man who had then laughed off promises of taking her away? She would have been very angry – and children could kill. She had certainly known Gabriel would be alone and unsuspecting in the churchyard. And when she'd been trapped last night, had she reached for a standard lie? I only found the body. Was that the direction in which Kerr was pushing him? Not the mother, not the father. The child. No, that's terrible. Find something else, not just because you want to, but because it makes sense.

Look at the little details, things that didn't seem important. There might be something . . . As Kerr followed Sally back into the room, Maltravers straightened up.

'Of course.'

He barely breathed the words, but Kerr still caught them. 'Of course what?'

'Give me a minute.'

Sally kept looking at him as she put the tray of coffee down, then they all waited as Maltravers silently continued to stare out of the window.

'Gus?' Tess prompted finally.

He turned towards Kerr. 'If you'd said "wild imagination", I might have got there sooner. But is it true?'

'Is what true?'

'You know what full well and fine because you were way ahead of me, weren't you?'

'Possibly,' Kerr agreed quietly. 'But I was hoping you'd see it for yourself. You have to admit that it makes sense.'

'Do Tess and I get to play this game?' Sally demanded.

'It's not a game,' Maltravers told her. 'It's why somebody murdered another human being.' He looked at Kerr again. 'But can it be proved?'

'Only if it's forced into the open, and then it should prove itself of course. There's not enough to take to the police yet and it's certainly not the sort of thing in which I wish to be involved. But perhaps you could do it. I have some suggestions on that . . .' He looked hesitant again. 'That is if they're of any use.'

'I'm sure they will be,' Maltravers told him.

Chapter Sixteen

Doreen Flyte's safe, secure, monotonous world had gone mad; not through some spectacular upheaval, but by tiny fragments suddenly no longer in place. First Gilbert had returned home, unannounced, from the bank in the middle of the day, trembling and agitated, refusing to let her call the doctor, even though he said he had felt unwell, then retreating to his study and remaining there for hours. His presence in the house had disturbed her own pedestrian, ordered life; she had felt unable to go for her customary walk in case he suffered some sort of attack. Her mother-in-law kept demanding what was the matter, subtly hinting that Doreen was not looking after her husband properly. Then Gilbert had gone back to work, only to return with the news that he was taking a few days' leave for no apparent reason. It was stupefying; his holidays were as fixed as religious festivals. Two weeks in June when they all went to the same hotel in Weston-super-Mare, a week in April and early November for gardening, three days in spring when he attended the annual conference of the Naval History Society. It was a pattern set in stone, like everything else in their lives. Now it had not just been cracked; Doreen felt that it had instantly crumbled and she was left with nothing but debris. Hesitant, timid questions had only made things worse; Gilbert, normally so reliable and certain, had become distracted, angrily demanding not to be pestered, impatient with her concern. His mother had started to sulk, muttering complaints, blaming her bewildered daughter-in-law, imagining horrifying explanations with almost gleeful gloomy satisfaction.

'His father went odd at the end and they found it was because of the tumour . . . they're going to make him redundant . . . he's been working too hard and I've warned him that he'd wear his brain out one day . . . they've got those computers in the bank now and I was reading only the other day that they give off some sort of rays that change people's personalities . . . he's always been sensitive, so I hope you haven't done anything to upset him . . .'

And as his wife silently screamed inside herself, Gilbert Flyte sat alone in his study, fear and anger breeding obsessive hatred. How dare this man interfere in matters that were none of his business? He had admitted that he had no official position; there should be a law against poking into people's private lives, whatever they might have done. He'd a good mind to . . . to what? Complain? Report him? Who to? And how could he do that without everything coming out? In Flyte's mind, Maltravers became like a bomb planted in the very foundations of his life, a bomb that had to be defused if he was not to live in perpetual terror of its detonation. And his tormented mind could think of only one way to remove it, desperate and frightening, but at least an escape from the danger closing in on him.

Swollen cumulus clouds were buffeted across Wedgwood sky and sweet chestnuts landed on the grass with tiny thuds as wind whipped the branches of the Lazarus Tree. Maltravers zipped up his bomber jacket as the first chill of autumn touched the afternoon.

'Is there anything I haven't thought of?' he asked.

'I don't think so.' Tess pushed back long flames of hair blown across her face. 'But you'll have to lie convincingly to Stephen.'

Maltravers smiled. 'What did Alex Kerr say? "A reputation for honesty is a liar's best weapon." Anyway, part of what I'm going to tell him is the truth.'

'But only part,' Tess added.

'Then let's hope it's enough.' He glanced up at St Leonard's church clock. 'He and Michelle will be home soon. We'll make ourselves scarce and get back around six. The Raven will be open then and we can take him there.'

They drove south out of the village and stopped on the crest

168

of the first rise of hills. As they walked along the edge of a field, the wind grew wilder and they took shelter in the lee side of an oak from where they could see Medmelton more than a mile away down the valley: touches of thatch and white walls, the church tower, protecting trees, the glittering ribbon of its little river. The sort of place where nothing ever happened.

Veronica watched grey smoke instantly disperse out of a pyre of dead leaves. It was one of those sometime jobs she had suddenly wanted to do; it took her out of the house and away from Stephen. He was deceiving her about Gus and that was totally unlike him. Why this reawakened interest in Patrick Gabriel's murder? Whatever the reason, she accepted that he would not have talked to her about it. She had always insisted that she was not interested and he knew her well enough to recognise an established no-go area. Normally, she would not have been concerned, but Veronica knew there was something happening behind Michelle's barriers and unless she could be sure that . . . a cloud of smoke was blown across her face and she blinked as it stung her eyes.

Through her kitchen window next door, Ursula stared at her sister-in-law. There was contentment. Self-assured and controlled, a mother now married to a caring man. A job she enjoyed. No inadequacies, no sense of failure, no agony of indecision. No guilt. As she looked down again at the half-peeled potato she was holding, she began to weep.

'So that's it.' Maltravers kept his voice lowered as he finished. There were not many people in the Raven, but Medmelton kept keen ears for strangers. Their arrival had been marked by suggestive nudges, nods and body movements and Tess had received especially interested looks, but there was no sense that she was recognised. 'I was right about Mildred Thomson.'

'The bloody . . .' Stephen shook himself. 'She's depraved! Wait till I get hold of her.'

'No,' Maltravers said sharply. 'Mildred knows she's been exposed so she'll almost certainly behave herself in future. And Michelle won't have anything more to do with her. She realises now how stupid she's been. I'm sorry to have had to break it to you about her and Gabriel, but that's a fait accompli.'

'I can live with that,' Stephen told him. 'I don't like it, but she's been putting it about for a long time. At least she didn't get pregnant or . . .' Alarm filled his face. 'The bastard didn't have Aids, did he?'

'He'd never have said anything if he had.' The possibility had not occurred to Maltravers. 'But that would surely have come out in the medical evidence at the inquest, and the press would have leapt on it. If it helps put your mind at rest, you could ask your doctor or the school medical officer to do a test. But I wouldn't worry about something that may not be true.'

Stephen swirled around the remains of his beer. 'And the murder?'

'What about it?' Tess watched carefully as Maltravers paused to light a cigarette. 'Michelle got mixed up with Mildred because Gabriel was dead, nothing to do with why he died. The best thing you can do is to forget the murder and concentrate on the fact that Michelle's been through a very bad time. She might not admit it, but she needs help.'

'She won't admit it . . . but what about your suggestion that it could have been her father who did it?' Stephen pressed.

Maltravers shrugged. 'It was never more than a suggestion. Perhaps I had too much time to think and began coming up with ludicrous ideas. Medmelton has that effect – at least it does on outsiders. But we don't know who he is, so it can never be proved and what the hell anyway?'

'You mean you're not bothered about who killed Gabriel?'

'Frankly, no. I wasn't exactly grief-stricken when I heard he was dead and I only took an interest because there could have been a connection with this churchyard business. Now I'm positive there never was. Murder's a police matter. Nothing to do with me.'

Stephen frowned at him. 'So you're forgetting it?'

'Of course I am.' Maltravers sounded surprised. 'You asked me here because you were worried about Michelle. I've managed to sort that out and the murder's irrelevant. If you want to find out any more, hire yourself a private detective . . . another drink?'

'My round.' Stephen started to stand up, then stopped. 'How much of this do I tell Veronica?'

'That's up to you,' Maltravers said. 'But Veronica can't have it all ways. You say she turned off before when something was worrying you about Michelle. She might do the same thing again. In your position I'd just be aware and see what happens. If Michelle starts to readjust herself, you can forget it. If it has long term effects, you'll have to make Veronica listen to you. Those are your family problems, friend.'

'Ain't that the truth?' Unexpectedly, Stephen smiled. 'I've got to thank you two and I ought to apologise. This wasn't the sort of visit you were expecting.'

Tess laughed. 'The last time I stayed in Devon I was bored out of my mind for a week. At least this time it's been interesting.'

'That's one word for it,' Stephen agreed drily. 'Back in a minute.'

Tess waited until he had reached the bar before speaking, her lips hardly moving. 'Your eyes change colour when you lie.'

'Do they? I can't see it from my side. How noticeable is it?'

'To me, a lot,' she replied. 'But I know you better than most.'

Maltravers looked towards the bar. 'But did I lie convincingly?'

'Oh, yes,' Tess assured him. 'Couldn't you see the relief on his face?'

'Yes, he . . . ah, ten past seven.'

'Pardon?'

'It's ten past seven. The precise Mr Flyte has just walked in. Don't stare, it makes him nervous.'

Tess resisted the impulse to look round, but kept her eyes fixed on the bar until Flyte entered her field of vision.

'With the dog? He looks innocuous.'

'They always do, but there are all sorts of nasty frustrations behind that boring exterior. Given just one kink of courage, that little man could be absolutely intolerable.'

*

In the rectory dining room, Bernard Quex finished the remainder of the previous night's cottage pie – he had never varied the recipe that his mother had taught him – and carried the plate through to the kitchen. There was a widower's adequate orderliness to his domestic life, basic diet supplemented by dishes prepared by concerned parishioners. That was how it had begun with Ursula; adultery out of a lamb casserole. If she had not done that, would he . . . ? As he shook water off the plate before putting it in the rack, he told himself he was seeking excuses again, trying to move the blame on to her, and despised his lack of honesty; sin could not be reconciled. She had not been the first and if it had not been her it would have been someone else.

He dried his hands and went into the hall, picking up the minutes of the Restoration Fund committee meeting from the table. For the next couple of hours he would be the respected rector and committee chairman, secret guilt and anguish masked by a charade that was a dream turned sour. As he walked through the darkened churchyard, seething wind shook the night and branches above his head creaked as though about to break.

Gilbert Flyte's fingers tightened round his glass as Maltravers's laugh rose above the chatter filling the Raven. Flyte had deliberately not looked round while he had been standing at his customary place, but there was a mirror behind the bar and he had seen Tess glance in his direction a couple of times, so apparently casual yet so obviously deliberate. Was Maltravers telling them the story of his confession, mocking him behind his back? He was despicable, confident and cruel, savouring his power. When he went back to London, he would tell everyone he knew about the man he had met in Medmelton who had fallen into his trap. And they would laugh at Gilbert Flyte and all he had achieved, his importance, his position, the regularity of his life, his weakness and his helplessness. The woman was laughing now, painted fingers pushing back shining red-bronze hair, subconsciously flaunting her beauty, arrogant as the man she was with.

But Flyte was not helpless, they underestimated him; they thought they knew him, but they were wrong. He was not going to let them destroy everything he had. He had passed through panic and begun to see what he had to do . . . and he would do it. They thought they could scare him, but all he needed was one opportunity. Just one moment when he would . . .

'On its way, Gilbert.'

'Pardon?'

Flyte twitched out of his reverie as the barmaid picked up his empty tankard and began to refill it.

'Your second pint. Don't tell me you don't want it. You always have the two.'

'Yes. Of course. Thank you.'

Flyte took a leather purse from his jacket pocket and handed her the money. The casual incident, which had happened hundreds of times before, was suddenly a reminder of the security of his existence among people who knew him, who he was convinced respected him. If Maltravers went to the police, there would be no more evenings in the Raven, no more meticulous scoring at cricket matches, no more taking the collection at St Leonard's, no more . . . no more anything. Reduced to such little matters, his way of life appeared very important and its preservation worth any risk.

Gilbert Flyte knew what he had to do. He finished his drink, said goodnight and left, carefully ignoring the table where Maltravers was sitting. Outside, he hurried alongside the green to his cottage, grateful that the rising violence of the night was keeping people indoors, and put Bobby in his car; the dog looked confused, but settled obediently on the back seat. Leaving one of the windows open, Flyte walked rapidly towards St Leonard's, a plan emerging in fragments. He rapidly searched among the graves until he found a heavy lead vase; the dead flowers it contained were hurled away by the wind as he tossed them aside. Then he crouched behind a tombstone from where he could see the Raven; it was nearly fifteen minutes before Maltravers, Tess and Stephen appeared, walking back towards the church, by which time Flyte had convinced himself there would be no problem with an alibi. He had left the pub at his usual time and Doreen was an obedient wife; he could persuade her to swear he had returned home a few minutes later and had not gone out again. All he had to do was to get Maltravers in the churchyard and wait for his opportunity in the darkness and confusion of the wild night . . . The hand gripping the vase began to tremble. As the three figures reached the lane by the ford, he crept deeper into the darkness behind the grave and licked cold dry lips before calling out.

'Hello!' Terror choked the cry in his throat and he swallowed hastily before shouting again. 'Hello! You there!'

Maltravers stopped. 'What was that?'

'What?' said Tess.

'Somebody shouted.'

'I didn't hear anything. It was the wind.'

'No, it wasn't. It sounded like "Hello". I think it came from over there.'

Tess clutched her coat as a sudden blast slapped the collar against her face. 'Who'd be in the churchyard on a night like this?'

'God knows, but I'm sure that . . . there it is again.'

'I heard it that time,' Stephen confirmed. 'It's not bloody Mildred, is it?'

'I don't imagine so,' Maltravers told him. 'It's probably just kids messing about.'

'Then we'd better look,' Stephen said grimly. 'One of them could be Michelle.'

'All right,' Maltravers agreed and turned to Tess. 'But you go on and check if she's at home.'

'What for?' she demanded. 'Whether or not she is, there's still someone in the churchyard. I'm coming with you.'

'OK.' Maltravers knew there was no point in arguing. 'But no wandering off. We all stay together just in case.'

'In case of what?'

'If I knew that, I wouldn't have to say we stay together.'

Flyte dared a quick look round the edge of the gravestone, then shrank back as he saw them moving in a group beyond the churchyard wall. Not all three! Just him! On his own and in the dark, unaware of what was going to happen. Like Patrick Gabriel had been. Perhaps they would split up . . . he heard one of them speak as they reached the lychgate. It was a situation in which he was not in control, where he had to make instant decisions and could not afford a mistake. He whimpered with fright, then suddenly leapt up and bolted from his hiding place.

'Who's that?'

The shout was snatched away by the wind as Flyte ran down the side of the church, starting to sob with fright as he heard running steps behind him. Cut off by the rectory and its neighbouring cottages, there was no way out from the back of St Leonard's. The wind surged angrily, buffeted in all directions as it crashed against the church walls. Flyte reached the clump of yew bushes, high, fat and holding their own deeper darkness. He plunged into them then stumbled across a barrel tomb, scrambled to his knees and crouched behind another gravestone. Gasping for breath, tear-blurred eyes instinctively recorded ancient carved lettering. 'Sacred to the memory of Thomas Smith, 1818–1902. And of his daughter, Faith, died 1845, aged three months. And of his wife Jane, 1830–1913. "Blessed art they who live in the fear of the Lord".' He strained his ears above huge gushes of wind, desperately trying to locate where his pursuers might be.

'Where's Tess?' Maltravers demanded as he and Stephen emerged at the back of the church.

'She ran round the other side. She must have thought whoever it is might have tried dodging us by doing the full circuit.'

'The stupid . . . Tess! Tess!' Fear shot through his shouting. 'We must find her before we do anything else. Come on.'

Stephen followed him as he ran towards the north side of St Leonard's, still calling Tess's name.

'Over here!' Her voice came from near the rectory.

'Where?' Maltravers shouted. 'We can't see you.'

'Here! By the bushes. I saw . . .' The wind crashed in again and drowned whatever else she was saying. Amid the yews, Flyte smothered a cry as he heard her within yards of his hiding place.

'Stay there!' Maltravers yelled. 'Don't move!'

Flyte heard racing footsteps coming nearer as he scuttled like a terrified animal in any direction that led away from danger. He reached a sprawl of brambles and realised that beyond them was the wall alongside the path to Dymlight Cottage. Thorns tearing his hands and face, he forced his way through them and crawled over the wall, falling into the ditch beyond it. The impact winded him and he lay weeping with pain, dread and helplessness. For one mad moment in his life, he had been driven by the urgency of crisis to believe he had courage. And now he was trapped and could only wait for his tormentors to discover him. Gilbert Flyte, deputy bank manager, Rotarian, church-warden, biographer, trembled as cold ditchwater begin to soak into his clothes.

'For Christ's sake, I told you to stay with us!' Maltravers's voice cracked with angry relief as he reached Tess.

'I'm all right!' she snapped back impatiently. 'Whoever it was went into these bushes. They could be anywhere by now.'

'Could they get out of the graveyard from here?' Maltravers asked Stephen.

'All they'd have to do is climb the wall.'

Maltravers jerked his head abruptly as a sudden scatter of stinging rain laced the wind lashing his face. 'That's all we need. Let's try anyway.'

They searched cautiously for several minutes, the rain increasing, before they gave up.

'There's nobody here,' Maltravers said. 'Or if they are, they're welcome to stay here. Let's forget it.'

'But who might it have been?' Stephen asked.

'I don't know and I don't care. From what I saw, it looked like a man, so you can stop worrying about Michelle. She's probably at home in front of the fire which is where we should be.'

Less than ten feet from where they were standing, Flyte painfully held panting breath. It was going to be all right. They hadn't recognised him in the darkness. As long as the ditch was deep enough for them not to see him as they walked past . . . he lay very still as he heard them hurrying up the lane. Then he forced himself to wait until he was certain they were indoors before cautiously peering out. Irrationally, he began to feel successful. He had deceived them and there might now be another opportunity, one that he could plan more carefully. He had proved to himself that he had the courage to do it, all it needed was more preparation. Perhaps he could . . . as he made his way home, Gilbert Flyte began to repair his shaming sense of humiliation by telling himself that next time . . . next time . . .

Maltravers and Tess heard St Leonard's clock strike one as the wind, now pitiless in its fury, howled around Dymlight Cottage.

'Who do you think it was?' Tess asked.

'In the churchyard? God knows. Perhaps someone was planning to steal the lead off the roof, although they must have been out of their minds on a night like this.'

'We might find out more in the morning.'

'Possibly.'

They lay in silence for a while, then Tess moved closer to him, pulling his arm across her. 'For comfort. Perhaps we're wrong.'

'Perhaps. And if we are, we can just go home and forget it. If I was the type who said prayers, I'd pray for that.'

Chapter Seventeen

Shrieking like a banshee, the wind scoured the valley with the fury of a living thing in pursuit of hidden quarry. Gusts buffeted outcrops of rock on the hillsides, probing frenzied fingers into granite crevices before dashing away to race among trees, frantically ransacking the mottled camouflage of dead leaves and whipping between trunks to flush out some fugitive. Occasionally it paused, chafing as if uncertain where to go next, then regathered and tore on, a raging army of phantom hounds howling under stampeding, death-grey clouds. Shaking roof tiles and hissing through thatch, it besieged Medmelton's cottages, rattling windows to demand entrance before swirling away in frustration. It threw columns of air down chimneys, billowing smoke vanguard of its invasion, or sent thin jets whistling through cracks beneath doors, chill, urgent and hostile. The lychgate of St Leonard's groaned as it swept into the churchyard, breaking in a violent, invisible wave against the west front.

Just after eleven o'clock in the almost empty lounge bar of the Raven, Maltravers watched the pub's hanging sign swing on its wooden post, helpless as a tattered sail in a storm-boiling sea. Broken twigs tumbled across the deserted green opposite and a wandering dog scampered for shelter. As he looked out, a lone figure appeared walking towards the pub, coat flapping like struggling wings, head bent against the blast. Maltravers returned to where Tess was sitting by the log fire crackling in the huge stone grate. As he sat down, she reached across the table and took his hand; staring at the drink in front of him, he returned the encouraging pressure of her fingers. Whichever way it went, the situation held too much human pain and . . . the wind howled in triumph, blasting cold through the room as the door opened. The handful of morning customers who had ventured out looked up as the newcomer stumbled inside then hurled his weight against the door to force it shut again. Captured whirling air was swallowed and died as the sanctuary within was re-established. The man stood for a moment, smoothing ruffled hair and unfastening his coat, then crossed to the fireplace.

'Thank you for coming,' Maltravers said. 'You've not met Tess.'

'No.' With automatic courtesy, Ewan Dean held out his hand. 'Hello.'

'What would you like to drink?' Maltravers asked.

'Oh . . . thanks. Just a half. Bitter.'

Tess nearly made some banal, instinctive remark about the weather as Maltravers went to the bar, but small talk would have been grimly farcical and Dean appeared to prefer silence. Their eyes met as he sat down, then he looked away again. She mentally played a writer's game which Maltravers often did on a train or walking down a crowded street; find the one adjective to describe a face. Frequently the features were a mask with nothing in the eyes or set of the mouth to draw on, but when personality or emotions were visible, the right word came. Melancholy, vulnerable, impish, distressed, cavalier, imperious, worldly, cynical. She sought the word for Ewan Dean's face: cautious . . . no, more than that . . . guarded. He made no gesture of thanks as Maltravers placed the beer in front of him.

'I didn't understand the note you pushed through my door last night,' he said. 'I only came because it said you wanted to talk about something serious.'

'Murder's serious,' Maltravers replied quietly as he sat down.

'Whose murder?'

'Patrick Gabriel's.'

'Gabriel? God, that was . . . it's all been forgotten.'

'Not by me it hasn't.'

'Well it has by me.' Dean swallowed half the contents of his glass and looked straight at Maltravers. 'And everybody else in Medmelton. I know you've been prying into it, but I can't see why it's any of your business. From what Stephen's told me, you couldn't stand Gabriel when he was alive. Why this sudden concern now he's dead?'

'Patrick Gabriel was a bastard,' Maltravers admitted. 'A talented one, but a bastard all the same. But my opinion doesn't mean that I think someone should have killed him.'

'And what's any of this got to do with me?'

'Everything. You're the one who did it.'

Tess stiffened as fury flashed across Dean's face and the knuckles on the glass he was holding went white. Then he controlled himself.

'I knew this was a waste of time.' He started to stand up. 'Thanks, but I won't finish your bloody drink.'

Maltravers ignored the reaction. 'And you killed him because he made love to your daughter.'

Half risen from the table, Dean stopped and was very still for a moment. Then he looked at Maltravers as though he was insane.

'What the hell are you talking about? I don't have a daughter. I don't have any children.'

'Yes you have,' Maltravers contradicted. 'And once I realised that, it explained a great deal. Michelle's your daughter – which of course is why Veronica has never admitted to anyone who the father was. It was her own brother.'

Dean leaned forward, angry fists resting on the table's edge. His self-control was now absolute.

'I'll just say this and then I leave. If you ever repeat that, I shall . . . no, I won't sue you. I'll kill you. Who the hell do you think you are, making accusations like that? Against my sister.'

'Back off, Ewan.' Maltravers sounded impatient. 'If you're going to kill me, it'll have to be here and now, because unless you sit down again and listen to me I'm going to the police. Then they'll investigate and stir up so much dirt that it'll stick to everybody. The first thing will be DNA fingerprinting of you and Michelle – and there'll be no refusals this time. I'm no scientist, but I know the results will prove you're her father. Do you want Michelle to know that? Do you want your parents to know? Think about it.'

Dean stared at him for a moment, then turned to Tess. 'How do you live with a madman?'

'I don't,' she replied. 'But I live with a man who sometimes has an eccentric view of the law. In his position, a lot of people wouldn't have asked you to meet them, they'd have gone straight to the police. Gus is actually offering a way out of this – at least for some people. And they're people that you love.'

She laid her hand on his right fist, still pressed against the table. 'Hear him out, Ewan. Please. When he's finished you can still walk out if you want to.'

Dean's fist hardened beneath her fingers, then began to slacken before he pulled it away. He breathed in very deeply, straightened his chair again and sat down.

'Go on.'

'Thank you.' Maltravers was aware that he had taken a very significant step. 'I'll make this as short as possible, because I can appreciate it's going to be painful for you. I could begin with when Patrick Gabriel came to Medmelton, but of course the real starting point was when you and Veronica became lovers . . .'

The rage that had appeared in Dean's eyes when Maltravers had first made the accusation had hardly faded; now it erupted again, but this time it was mingled with grief and confusion.

'Don't interrupt,' Maltravers said. 'That's none of my business or anybody else's. It's illegal, but it happens more often than many people think and human emotions don't take much notice of laws. Nobody else was hurt by what happened and it's obvious that you and Veronica are still very close to each other. I'm counting on the fact that you love her.

'Anyway, it happened and both of you kept your secret. And then you married and couldn't have children and had to watch your daughter grow up without being able to acknowledge her. For a long time, you could sublimate your feelings by being a favourite uncle, but then Veronica married Stephen. He's a good stepfather, but he was another man taking over what you wanted to be your role in Michelle's life.'

'I can see how you make a living as a writer,' Dean interrupted. 'You've got the imagination for it. Can you prove any of this?'

'Not a word,' Maltravers admitted. 'But are you going to risk telling me to get lost and hope I won't go to the police?'

'Would you?' Dean challenged.

'You'd better believe it.'

'So you don't give a damn about how much pain you'd cause.'

'If I didn't give a damn, I'd have gone to them already. Wouldn't I?'

Dean made no reply and the silence between them was startlingly invaded as a broken tree branch smashed against the window, cracking the glass like a pistol shot. For a few moments, there was an alarmed agitation, the landlady rushing to examine the damage, the wind whipping in again as a man suddenly anxious for his greenhouse hastily left, and what sounded like schadenfreude comments were made about the state of the church roof. Hidden behind the bar, the landlord's dog whimpered.

'Wouldn't I?' Maltravers repeated quietly as relative peace returned to the room. Dean had remained so totally still during the disturbance that it might never have happened.

'I don't know you well enough to say. Perhaps you would.'

'And if I did – because you left me no option – would I be right?'

Dean looked at him without replying for a very long time. Then he seemed to reach a decision.

'You've been asking questions, but you haven't got anywhere, so for some reason you've come up with this and are trying to trick me into confessing something by threatening to go to the police with it. But you're bluffing.'

'Then call it.' Maltravers picked up his glass and finished his wine. 'Tess and I are going back to Dymlight Cottage – we've already packed incidentally. We'll be leaving Medmelton at . . .' he glanced at the clock above the bar, 'let's say twelve o'clock. If you don't come to talk to me before then, I go to the police. That's the best part of an hour for you to think things over. Sorry, Ewan, but it's as simple as that.'

Gaze fixed on the crackling fire, Dean remained motionless as they stood up and walked out. Tess clutched Maltravers's arm tightly as they bowed their heads into the shredding wind.

'Do you think he'll come?' She had almost to shout over the tumult.

'I don't know,' Maltravers gasped back. 'But I hope so.'

In the Raven, a man at the bar called across to Dean. 'What was all that about, Ewan? That was Stephen Hart's friend you were talking to. Gus . . . whatever it is. The one who's been asking bloody questions.'

'I was just saying goodbye,' Dean replied. 'He's leaving today.'

'Good riddance . . . want the other half?'

'No thanks. I've got to go.'

It was only after he left that someone wondered why he had not been at his shop that morning.

In Exeter, Veronica was completing an application form for a local authority grant when she was overwhelmed with an inexplicable sense of disaster. The pen suddenly refused to move across the paper and her hand shook; for a few seconds she felt icy cold and physically sick as the office went blurred. The moment passed and she realised that she was frightened, because . . . because . . .

'Ewan?' Instinctively whispered, the name terrified her. 'What's the matter?'

Dear God, this hadn't happened for years, this instant agonising *knowing* that something was wrong. What was it? An accident? Violent illness? Danger? She snatched up the telephone and dialled the model shop; it only rang twice before she heard her brother's voice.

'Dean's Model Centre . . .'

'Ewan! It's . . .'

'. . . I'm afraid we're closed at the moment, but if you leave your name and number after the . . .'

Frantically, she rang off and began to dial his home number. It was past eleven, why wasn't he at work? Ursula should have called her if . . .

'Come on . . . come *on!*' she begged as the ringing tone remorselessly echoed itself. Ursula must be in on a foul morning like this . . . unless she'd gone to see Bernard about something to do with the church. Veronica dropped the receiver on her desk and pulled open a drawer, dragging out a directory. Quayle ... Queen ... Quentin ... Quex. Holding the number in the turmoil of her mind with constant repetition, she punched it in ... Christ, an ansaphone again.

Now the knowing had hardened into total conviction, heightened into terror of what it might be. Snatching up her handbag, she raced out of the office, all self-control lost, crying some meaningless explanation about a crisis at home to startled colleagues. Outside on the pavement, she stopped as she realised that Stephen had the car, then ran towards the taxi rank by the railway station. Reading a newspaper, the driver in the first cab jumped as she banged on his window.

'Medmelton! Drover's Cottage. Near the church. Please, it's very urgent! There's been ... there's been an accident!'

She leapt into the back as he dropped the paper and started the engine. 'Fast as I can, lady,' he promised. 'Serious, is it?'

'Yes.'

But she still didn't know what it was, only that Ewan was sending some urgent message on the private channel of communication they had shared all their lives.

Dymlight Cottage held only waiting silence. Tess had found an executive toy on top of the desk and was forcing her attention on to guiding a blob of mercury to the centre of a maze; sitting in front of the fireplace, Maltravers stared at the display of dried flowers. Both of them stirred uneasily as the granddaughter clock sounded the half hour.

'There's still plenty of time.' Tess looked uncertain as Maltravers made no reply. 'Gus, are you sure about what you're doing? If you're wrong ...'

'But I'm not,' he contradicted. 'If I was, Ewan would have either laughed in my face, hit me, or called the police himself and asked them to charge me with blackmail or threatening behaviour or ... well, something. He was about to walk out when I first said it, but he sat down again and listened. Then I knew.'

'All right,' Tess agreed. 'But if he doesn't come and admit it, do you really have to go to the police? It's going to cause so much hurt – and would it be worth it for Patrick Gabriel?'

'Not really,' he admitted. 'But that's not the point. If Ewan's killed one man because he loves his daughter so much, will he stop there? Say Michelle married and her husband beat her up or cheated on her? Suppose Stephen were to start treating her in a way that Ewan didn't like? If we leave this alone, I don't like to think he'd kill again – but he might.'

'And there's no other way to sort it out?'

'If there is, I wish I could see it.' He rubbed his eyes. 'Christ, I'm tired. Look at it from Michelle's point of view. If Ewan admits killing Gabriel, she has a murderer for an uncle. But if I have to go to the police, the truth about her birth comes out – and she has a murderer for a father. Which is worse?'

Tess looked down at the toy she was still holding, then shook it so that the mercury shattered into drops. Turning the toy on its side made it into a complete blob again – but it was still outside the maze.

'And will you find a way through?' she whispered sadly.

'Pardon?' Maltravers said.

'It doesn't matter.'

The silence returned for a few minutes, then they heard someone run up the path and fumble a key in the front door. Maltravers twisted round in his chair. Ewan could well have a key for Dymlight Cottage, but why was he suddenly . . . ? The door opened and Veronica burst in.

'Gus! Have you seen Ewan anywhere? He's not at home and . . . and . . . and there's something wrong!' Wind howled through the open door behind her.

Maltravers leapt up. 'What do you mean, wrong? What's happened?'

'I don't . . . I just know that . . . I can't explain. But I have to find him. Have you seen him?'

'We were talking to him in the Raven about half an hour ago. He was still there when . . . hang on!' But Veronica had raced out of the house.

'Let her go!' Tess ordered as Maltravers started to follow her. 'If he's still there, they can talk to each other. If he's not, she'll come back here.'

'But what's going on?' Maltravers demanded. 'Why's she suddenly turned up?'

'Because somehow she knows that something serious has happened,' Tess replied. 'But he can't have rung her or she wouldn't have dashed in here looking for him. That means . . . God alone knows, but she and Ewan are very, very close and strange things happen in Medmelton. The question is, what do we do now?'

Maltravers was still trying to analyse the situation. 'I assumed he must have called her . . . but you're right. If he had, she wouldn't be panicking about where he was. So it's . . . ESP or some form of contact between people I don't understand.'

'There's a great deal you don't understand.'

Tess and Maltravers whirled round as the voice spoke behind them. Ewan Dean had let himself in through the back of the house and was standing in the kitchen doorway. 'I know why she's here. Each of us has always known when the other one's in trouble. We don't have to make any effort to communicate with each other, it just happens. In the circumstances, I should have expected it.'

'Will she know any details?' Maltravers asked cautiously.

'No, it's just a very strong feeling. That's enough.' Dean smiled sourly. 'She's going to find out anyway, isn't she? I realised you weren't bluffing in the Raven and I could see exactly how bad it would be if . . . I just needed time to come to terms with it. If I don't go to the police, then you will. It's better that I do it.'

Maltravers nodded. 'The other night – it doesn't matter why – I told Michelle she was a very brave girl. I can see where she gets it from.'

'I'm not sure how brave it is to take the only way out there is.'

'Oh, it can be,' Maltravers said. He turned to Tess. 'Veronica'll be back in a moment. Go and wait for her. See if the church is open and take her in there . . . I'm afraid you're going to have to tell her.'

'I know that.' Tess was already stepping outside. Maltravers shut the door and the wind went out of the room.

'Will she be able to handle it?' Dean asked. 'Telling Veronica.'

'Yes. Perhaps it'll be better coming from a stranger.'

'I have to see her before I leave.'

'Of course . . . and what about your wife?'

'That doesn't matter.' Now the adjective for Ewan Dean's face was resigned. 'Just tell me how you knew. Veronica can't have let anything slip and nobody else could have told you.'

'Nobody told me anything, certainly not Veronica,' Maltravers confirmed. 'It was nothing more than guesswork. The first thing was that I realised Gabriel must have been messing about with Michelle. Later on, she confirmed it.'

'How?' Dean demanded. 'She'd never have talked to you.'

'Not normally,' Maltravers admitted. 'But . . . well let's say that something happened that made her admit it. It doesn't matter what it was. At the time I had a theory that the killer could have been her father, who might have seen them together in the churchyard, but I couldn't see a way of discovering who he could be. I won't bore you with my wild guesses, but it finally struck me that if there's a clear view into the churchyard from upstairs in this cottage, then it must be the same next door. And if it was you, it explained why Veronica had never admitted who Michelle's father was. I'd already been told that you and Veronica were very close when you were young – you had a reputation of being the protective older brother.

'So that gave a motive, and I also knew you had the opportunity. On the night of Gabriel's murder you and Ursula came to see Stephen and Veronica and stayed late. That would have delayed Michelle going out to meet him and she'd have had to wait a while after you left. So that must have been when you went out and killed him . . . how did you know they were going to meet that night?'

'When I came home from work that day, they were talking to each other by the lychgate so it seemed a reasonable possibility. I'd found out what was going on about a week earlier when I couldn't sleep one night and . . . I don't know . . . looked out of the window for something to do.' Remembered pain filled Dean's face. 'You don't have children, do you?'

'No.'

'Then you can't know how it felt. I nearly followed him to his cottage there and then, but I'm not the type to act emotionally. I knew I'd probably leave evidence. I was still thinking about how I could do it when I saw them that evening.'

'And after you killed him, you stole his poetry,' Maltravers added.

'I had to. Stephen had told me what Gabriel said he was writing about and there could have been something in it that might identify Michelle. I daren't risk that.'

'And was there?'

'Do you think I bothered to look? I took everything I could find – at least he was tidy and his notebooks were all together on a table – and put them in my car. Next day the whole lot went into the central heating boiler at the shop. I didn't read any of it. I didn't give a shit that I might be robbing English literature of some masterpiece.'

'I don't imagine you did,' Maltravers agreed. 'But weren't you worried that Michelle would find him later that night?'

'By the time we left here, I reckoned she'd decide it was too late and . . .' Dean stopped and looked startled. 'Are you telling me she did?'

Maltravers had realised his mistake before the question was asked and knew he had to lie; Dean was going to suffer enough without knowing he had exposed his daughter to the sight of a murdered man.

'Of course I'm not,' he said. 'I wouldn't know that anyway, but you must be right. She'd have had to wait a while after you left and by that time she'd have assumed he'd gone home. He wasn't the patient type. The amazing thing is that he was still there when you met him.'

'She can't have gone.' Dean spoke as though he needed to convince himself, and Maltravers changed the conversation before he thought about it too much.

'What reason are you going to give the police for the murder?' he asked. 'They'll want a motive.'

Dean shrugged indifferently. 'You know what Gabriel was like. I'll tell them that after we left here I saw him in the church-yard and went to find out what he was doing. He was drunk and I'd had a few and we started arguing. Then he said something that made me lose my temper – I'll throw in some story about us having had a row before. The weapon's no problem – I carry my model-making knife with me most of the time – and I slashed out at him, realised what I'd done and kept quiet about it. If they want evidence, I've still got the knife. I cleaned it up of course, but there still might be something they can find to clinch it from that. Perhaps they'll be able to prove it matches the wound.'

He smiled cynically. 'Let's remember, this is going to be a genuine confession as far as it goes. And I'll want to help them prove it.'

'And why will you suddenly be admitting it after all this time?'

'Remorse? Guilt? Can't live with my conscience any longer?' Dean gave a hollow laugh. 'You know I can lie convincingly. I'll make sure the police believe me and they'll be happy to wrap it up. Don't worry. I accept that I'm going to jail. It's better than the alternatives.'

Maltravers nodded sympathetically. 'The book of etiquette doesn't cover this situation. Just believe me when I say I don't get any satisfaction out of this. I wish I'd never got involved.'

'You're not the only one,' Dean told him. 'Look. I want to get this over with now, but I have to see Veronica.'

'I know you do. Go home and I'll tell her you're there.'

As he walked past the Lazarus Tree, he saw the two women sitting in the church porch. Tess stepped outside to speak to him.

'The church is locked,' she explained. 'I've told her and had a hell of a job keeping her here at first, but now she's switched off. I can't get through to her and God alone knows what she's thinking.'

'Let me try. He's admitted it.'

Resentful and accusing, only Veronica's Medmelton eyes moved as Maltravers approached her, uncanny as eyes blinking in a portrait.

'Ewan wants to talk to you,' he said. 'He's at his cottage.'

She stood up without a word and started to walk past them as though they were not there.

'I'm sorry, Veronica,' Maltravers added. 'I . . .'

'Don't say anything.' Her voice was bitter as acid. 'You've caused enough pain.'

Tess gave a little sob and took hold of his arm as they watched her walk away. 'You didn't deserve that, but Christ, she's hurting. Just take me away from here now.'

'We must tell Sally what's happened before we go.'

'All right,' she agreed. 'But then I want out . . . oh, but what about Stephen? He's going to come home and find that we've gone and all hell's broken out. What's he going to think?'

'Hopefully nothing. He'll find my note saying that something urgent has cropped up and we had to get back to London in a hurry. The fact that Ewan has admitted the murder will put our departure in the shade.'

'And will he? Admit it?'

'I've not left him any choice.'

Tess crossed her arms and wrapped them tightly against her body. 'I tried everything I could with Veronica, Gus. But there were no words. I wanted to hug her and give her lots of strokes and . . . just *reach* her.' She began to cry softly. 'But I couldn't.'

'Nobody ever can. We know that well enough.' Maltravers put his arm round her. 'But we also know she's a survivor. Come on . . . Medmelton never wanted us here in the first place.'

The Old Cottage
Beddowes Lane
Medmelton
October 15th

Dear Gus and Tess,

As you can imagine, it's been nightmarish here, but at last I've found a space to write and tell you what's happened. You must have seen the press reports that Ewan has been charged and is being held in custody; the trial will be at Exeter Crown Court, but the date hasn't been fixed yet. His father suffered a mild heart attack when he heard, but everyone's rallied round magnificently. Medmelton may be unfriendly towards strangers, but we look after our own.

Veronica is – well, Veronica. I met her outside the stores the other morning and when I mentioned Ewan, I don't have the words to describe the look on her face. I felt so dreadfully sorry for her. She did talk a little about Michelle. I'd heard she'd had some sort of breakdown, but Veronica said she's going back to school next week and – ironic this – Ursula has been a great help to her; it's as though what's happened has brought them together. Incidentally, I'm fairly certain that the affair with Bernard is over. I'm not positive, but it feels that way somehow.

Stephen came to see me a few days after you left and said he wanted to thank me for my part in sorting out the Mildred Thomson business. He hasn't told Veronica anything about it of course, particularly in view of what's happened with Ewan. He (Stephen) was shattered about that and is obviously doing all he can to support her – not the easiest of tasks. More importantly, he clearly doesn't know the full story; they've kept their secret. I expect he'll already have written to you.

Mildred is much as the same, at least on the surface. I have my suspicions about her and a couple of kids in the village and I'm going to have to find a way to drop a discreet word to their parents; but that's Medmelton business and you mustn't worry about it. Gilbert Flyte cornered me in the Raven last night and started asking if I knew if you were coming back. When I told him I didn't think so, he said, 'I hope you're right,' then muttered something about people interfering in things that weren't their business. He's obviously still scared stiff that you're going to blow the whistle on him, but he can sweat on it.

It's difficult to say what the general reaction is. Some people seem almost offended, as if Ewan has let the village down by not continuing to keep quiet after so long. I can't be doing with it, but Medmelton's home and you make the best of it.

Somehow I can't imagine you'll want to come here again, but I get up to London from time to time and perhaps we can meet. Alex sends his best wishes; we both agree that only an outsider could have sorted it all out. I hope it didn't hurt too much.

Much love to you both,
Sally Baker